Raven Pirate

Assassin Spy

By
Landra Graf

Copyright © 2016 by Landra Graf
ISBN: 978-1-61333-949-7
Cover art by Tibbs Designs

Published by Decadent Publishing Company, LLC
Look for us online at:
www.decadentpublishing.com

Praise for Raven Pirate Assassin Spy

Raven, Pirate, Assassin, Spy is a fantastic blend of action and intrigue with enough sexual tension to make your e-reader smoke! ~ Catherine Peace, author

Smart and sexy, Raven Pirate Assassin Spy *is a delightful romp through an alternate history of the second World War, involving flying pirate ships, the technology of Nicola Tesla, and a mysterious captain trying to hide her secret identity. Sorella Corvino is a gift of a heroine—deadly, brilliant, and determined— and it's a treat to watch her hard edges melt away as she falls in love with the man she least expects to care about. Definitely one you won't be able to put down!* ~ The Book Princess

Dedication

To LS, CP, LE, MM, and AL - you lift me up and keep me writing.

To my daughter, Future Rockstar, you can read this when you're older.

To my husband, thank you for supporting me, even when the idea sounds crazy.

To my son, Detective Masterbuilder, dreams can come true… snuggle snuggle puffle puff.

~A Note from Landra~

Hello Readers,

Thank you for reading *Raven Pirate Assassin Spy*. From the moment I was assigned my fairytale I knew this book would take place in an alternate history, specifically a history where Germany won the first world war and Nikola Tesla wasn't a pacifist. From there it didn't take much to arrive at my headstrong heroine, Sorella and her journey to find her brother. This book was a joy to write, research, and create. I hope you get lost in the world as much as I did.

Of course I'd love to know what you think and if you believe there's room for another story. Tell me everything at <u>landra.graf7@gmail.com</u>

Prologue

New Orleans
1936

Gretchen pulled the scratchy half-blanket tight around her shoulders and took a step closer to the fire, a small orange blaze inside a busted metal pot. What little heat came out warmed her bare legs, her threadbare cotton dress barely coming past her knees. She didn't have long, mere minutes, before mother noticed her gone, snuck off to hear the storyteller again. Except he wasn't on the small stool set against the wall like normal. If he didn't appear soon, she'd have to leave.

"Please," she whispered, her breath visible in the chilled night air blowing in from the coast.

The answer to her plea—a cat's loud howl. Startled, she looked away from the fire.

"Come for a tale, little one?" He squatted onto the stool, no taller than her. He'd a long beard, gray and grizzled, like the tangles of wires her older brother tried to straighten. His voice was scratchy; her mother said it happened because the storyteller loved to puff on the steel pipe he kept in his jacket pocket.

"Yes, Nicodemus." She loved his stories, the tales he'd share. It didn't matter if they were real or not; they gave her something to think about besides being tired or hungry.

"Then gather close. Warm yourself by the fire, wee one. For a gift, I'll tell you one of my favorites."

Searching, Gretchen looked all around, down at

the ground, over her shoulder. What could she give, for she had nothing? Then she leaned in and pecked a kiss on his wrinkly cheek.

He smiled. "Thank you. You'll need a special tale for such a special gift." He stroked his beard, eyes focused on the flames licking the air in front of them. "Once upon a time, there lived a girl born to parents who'd prayed for a daughter but never expected one."

"Was she special?"

Nicodemus tapped her hand with two fingers. "So special a band of thieves kidnapped her when she was a tiny thing, not much younger than you are. Her parents had no choice but to trade her brother in exchange for her safe return. The girl's future would crown her the queen of a kingdom upon her wedding day. With black hair, pale skin, and eyes as deep blue as the Mediterranean Sea, she'd be Europe's true jewel."

"I've never been to the Meditearret…Med… the sea."

"Why would you? It's thousands of miles away, and you have the Gulf right at your fingertips. You have no doubt seen the water that washed along those shores, for it travels long distances over time, more so than people." He chuckled. "Now, do you want to hear the rest?"

"Yes." She blushed. Even her mother said she always spoke too soon, no hesitation.

"The would-be princess didn't want her throne and ran away, searching for her lost brother and hoping to rescue him like he had saved her all those years ago."

Gretchen put her hand to her chest, trying to rub out the ache the story put there. To care about someone so much, to be cared for—

"Greta-girl!" Her mother's high-pitched yell echoed down the alleyway.

She ignored the call and looked back at Nicodemus, who puffed on his pipe, curls of smoke wafting into the air. Tugging on his coat sleeve, she asked, "Where is the princess?"

Before he uttered a reply, a hand clasped around her arm and yanked. With her free hand, her mother cuffed the back of her head. "I've been looking everywhere for you. Left your brother to do your work for you? We'll see how you like not eating then."

Gretchen rubbed her eyes to keep the tears from flowing.

Mother spat on the ground at Nicodemus's feet. "Stories." The word sounded like something cursed. "A bunch of drivel and a waste of time. Back to work, girl."

The words came with a shove to Gretchen's back, and she nearly fell, face first, as she took those few stumbling steps forward. Somehow she managed to stay upright and start the trek back to the busy main roads. The roads where her mother searched for a buyer, where she'd have to worry about being sold, and where no would save her.

Chapter One

Pontevedra, Spain
1936

Sorella Corvino only made promises she kept. So when she told the crumb in the next cell, "Once I get out of here, I'm going to kill you," those were words of truth, not fiction.

The evil bastard leaned forward, mere inches from the bars, and grinned. "I prefer my bits handled by a gorgeous dish, but, in a pinch, you'll do." His six yellowed teeth stabbing up through pinkish-white gums were a stark contrast to his soot-colored skin and graying eyes, the gray no doubt a product of the drugs and rotgut sold on every corner in Pontevedra. No one escaped the filth and poison festering in the streets of every European city unscathed.

"In your dreams." She stepped toward him, eyes narrowed. Maybe she wouldn't wait until she got out.

"That's what your girl is dreaming of tonight. Me and my co—"

She slid her hand between the bars and grasped the part of his anatomy he wanted to talk about in every other sentence, effectively cutting him off. Her grip firm, he started to drop. The cell wall made it impossible for her hand to follow without getting burned by the electric current pulsing through the bars. Even now, the hairs on her arm stood up, and she let go before her skin touched electrified metal.

4

"Bitch!" he howled, clutching at himself, his black dreads spread across the cell floor like brittle, charred ropes.

"You deserve that and a whole lot more." She rubbed her arm to clear away the lingering static electricity. What she wouldn't give her for a Tesla coil gun or an electo wand right now. The damn jailers took everything, even her balisong knives—all three pairs. They'd had fun searching her, treating her like a female toy, though they were bored after a few touches. She tugged on her buckskin pants to expel the memory.

So much for putting into port and getting a job. The idiot in jail with her had ruined all her good intentions of securing a contract by attempting to rape one of her crew. She'd jumped on him as soon as she'd heard Lila, the doctor's nurse, call out. Her first mate, Bastille, had seen to the girl, removing her from the scene while Sorella took out the threat. She'd almost accomplished the task until a bystander hit her with a bottle and got a reward for turning in two "disrupters of the peace."

How am I getting out of here? Like all good questions, hers was answered by the unexpected. The jail door at the top of the stairs opened, and an unconscious guard rolled down into the dark keep. Her rescuer took each step with care, no light illuminating the way. Yet, it wasn't another jailer or Bastille. Each heeled touch to wood let out a short metal *snick*. She'd never heard such a thing before.

She nearly shouted, but her jailmate did the work for her.

"Who's there?" The question came out as grizzled

as he looked.

No response, besides those measured, clinking steps. As she searched the dark, the mystery person came into view. Boots, pants, and a long jacket, not enough light to determine the color. Then the glint of a revolver at the waist, courtesy of the small trail of moonlight filtering through the tiny hole of a window at the top of the concrete wall behind her. She failed to make out much more than a male upper body with a square-jawed face, and…he wasn't looking at her.

The invader hunched down next to the collapsed guard and placed two fingers at his neck, no doubt ensuring the fool was dead. The intruder's hair was shorter than the poorer classes usually wore it, which bespoke money, yet his clothes of leather, un-shined, weren't fine.

He stood up, straightened his belt, and positioned himself in front of the other cell. "Tuul Machenk?"

"Yes." The scum had a name and, surprisingly, claimed it.

"*The Cursed* have a bounty on your head. You're coming with me."

She couldn't let that happen. Not now. "Wait a minute." Stepping toward the cell corner, Sorella armed herself with her most compelling feature, a smile. "You can't kill him. I've already told him he'd die by my hands. Let me kill him, and you can have the body."

"Look here, pretty lady. He's wanted alive." He unhooked an electo wand from his belt. "So we'll be leaving without a drop of blood spilt."

One problem solved. Now she'd need him to help her solve the other difficulty—finding *The Cursed*.

6

"Fine. Then let me help you."

"How do you figure on doing that?" His lips slightly tilted, like he wanted to smile and seemed to be trying his best not to. All the while, his fingers and palm worked the dial at the wand's base.

"Do you have a plan to get him out of here?" She raised both eyebrows challenging him. Sure he'd knocked out one guard, but there were more where that one came from. Not to mention street hawkers who'd love to get checkers for stopping escapees. "Because, if you don't, I sure do."

***

When Ian Marshall first walked into the jail, he'd expected a fight. Yet only one sentry stood on duty, one guard, a boy more than a man, for someone *The Cursed* claimed was too dangerous to be left to his own devices.

The rolling down the stairs bit had been an accident. To make sure he hadn't killed the kid, he checked for a pulse. It was there, but thready. No time to get the fool medical help.

Turning his attention toward the cells, he'd sized up his bounty, a grizzled, more-bone-than-flesh man who stood a few inches shorter and possessed eyes with more intelligence than he let on.

Ian hadn't planned on the feisty, mysterious woman in the other cell. She smiled. A perfect, white-toothed smile signaling trouble. Teeth like that rarely existed in war-ravaged Europe. Those who had them were in society's upper echelons, and if you were found with a rare, flawless pearl set, you'd be claimed and sold. Hell, he'd seen men kill to possess a person with unspoiled teeth.

He refused to mess with such a problem. Nope, he'd split with the bounty he came for and leave Trouble in her cell. She'd asked if he had a plan, but it didn't matter that she'd caught him flying by the seat of his cross seams. With a will came a way, and surviving the past few years had taught him he'd always find a way. So he ignored her.

"Step back, and I'll get you out of there." He finished setting the electo wand to EMP.

Tuul grinned in response. The man wasn't going to do a damn thing he said. Thankfully, he had a backup plan. He reached into his pocket and gripped the collar stuffed inside. He'd have to move fast.

The wand touched the bars. The current running through them sparked and then died. Switching to the heat setting allowed him to melt the lock. Once the lock was melted, his target charged the door with a growl. Ian stepped back and readied for the impact, moving himself out of the door's swinging path and removing the collar from his pocket.

Before the bastard could reach him though, the girl burst between them, shoving her fist into Tuul's face and knocking him back into the cell.

"What the hell are you doing?"

She marched forward into the cell, stomping on the prostrate man's bits with her boot heel. "Killing the scag like I promised him I would."

"Wait! Let's talk about this."

"What's to talk about?" she asked, wrapping Tuul's dreadlocks around her hand.

No time like the present to be charming, especially

since she'd exposed the scag's neck and looked ready to snap it. "Who are you, and why do you want this man dead?"

The questions put a halt to her actions. "I'm the captain of the *Liberté*, and this man tried to rape one of my crew."

Hard to argue against revenge when the scumbag deserves it. Then another thought came to mind. "Captain, eh?"

She cocked her head to the side. "Yes, what of it?"

"He," Ian pointed at the scag, "is worth a lot to *The Cursed*. You've heard of them?"

If she hadn't, she wasn't a true sky captain.

"Hasn't everyone?"

"All right, you give us a ride, and I give you part of the reward." She didn't need to know the payment involved his freedom and not coin. His little deception could be solved later, as long as he got her to release the man and secure the collar on him. Hopefully, they'd negotiate, or at least strike a temporary truce. Their immediate problem of getting out of the area without getting caught would be solved by her accepting his offer.

Shaking her head, she dropped the ropes of hair in her hand and stepped toward him. "Give me the choker."

"So you'll do it?" He extended the shock collar to her.

Taking the choker, she eyed him for a moment as if trying to decide whose neck to slap the damn thing on. As quickly as the thought, whatever it had been, ran through her head, it disappeared, and, a few swift movements later, the clasp clicked closed.

Only then did the bounty begin to show signs of life. Moaning and rubbing his eyes, fingers slipping up to touch the thick metal encased around his trunk, wires entwined around it. Ian knew the feeling of helplessness coupled with desperation when the realization hit that the collar couldn't be removed.

Trouble looked at him. "You'd better turn the damn thing on. Let's fly the coop."

"Right." He snatched the controller from his pocket and shoved his momentary compassion aside. The would-be rapist didn't need sympathy, and they needed to get out before a guard change. He flipped the blue switch on the small black box in his palm. Hard to believe Tesla's great technology had been used to develop objects designed to inflict pain on others, but Tesla had done what he needed to survive. Better to be the one with the box than the one locked in the device.

He asked the bounty, "Are you ready to leave?"

"Bollocks if I'm going with you." He coughed, gave up on removing his new jewelry, and sank to his knees.

"Well, you don't have much choice."

As soon as the bounty put palms to the cell floor and moved to stand, Ian tapped the control button. The reaction was instantaneous. Tuul flipped to his back, trembling from the momentary voltage winding its way through each limb.

"Now, do you understand?" Marshall stepped into the cell, not missing Trouble's smile at her enemy's weakened position.

"Oy, I understand. It's death here, and a chance to kill her if I go with you." Tuul looked back at

Trouble, whose gleaming eyes expressed her longing to end him, which would be unacceptable to Luther. For whatever reason, the bounty was worth more alive than dead.

"If you're so eager for a pass, come along," she replied, and headed for the stairs.

Ian offered a hand to his prone captive, but his assistance was rebuffed with a slap. The bounty rose on his own and followed the woman—who'd either get them out of Spain or get them caught.

***

Sorella's plan worked like all her plans—exactly as she had expected it to. This bounty hunter's poor execution of his mission, not to mention his failure to knock out the scag before he disarmed the cells, showed he lacked experience. Definitely no triggerman, but she saw potential in him despite his less than stellarly executed capture. Besides his looks, a way with words appeared to be his most valuable feature so far. Too bad words and a smile weren't needed to get them through the city streets and to her ship.

He didn't know it, yet, but teaming up with her would be one of his better choices, and after he led her to *The Cursed*, she'd toss him then rid the world of the scag who had tried to attack her crew.

Once upstairs, she retrieved her balisongs, coil gun, and electo wand, silently lifting praise as her hands touched each possession and placed it in its proper place on her person. Outside, the city was surprisingly silent, a shock since bad behavior never tended to sleep in Europe these days.

"Keep your heads down, and follow me," she whispered, crouching next to the mortar walls near the city square. Less than a kilometer away, the *Liberté* sat anchored, ready to launch as soon as she arrived.

Tuul and the hunter followed quietly. Thankfully, they were stealthy except for that small metal jingle on the heels of the hunter's boots.

Her father and teachers had told her often, "Perfection can only be sought by oneself and not others," but she'd failed to follow the lesson closely. In some ways, it made her a better captain, and in others….

She stopped mid-step, and the hunter bumped into her. The connection was like an errant spark from an electo wand, and one she was ignoring. "You need to silence your shoes," she hissed.

"No time. No one's around to hear them anyway," he growled, and pointed in front of her. "Keep going."

As she opened her mouth to reply, an alarm sounded in the distance. Out of time, she took off in a dead sprint toward the docks, hauling the metal whistle from the rope at her neck to her lips to announce her arrival.

Three trills and a tweet. *Your captain arrives.*

A metal shriek rent the air as the boarding deck opened, and the disc platforms, suspended on metal-infused ropes, descended. Two were empty, and Bastille waited on the third.

"We board and launch immediately."

Her first mate eyed the men beside her and

nodded.

Sorella turned, grabbing an empty platform and shoving it toward the hunter. "You on this one. Scag, the other."

"What about you?"

The question made her pause. When was the last time a man had worried about her or even thought to have cause? She linked an arm with her first mate and slipped a boot between his larger ones on the disc. "I ride with him."

The hunter's mouth slackened, his eyes narrowing. He looked dismayed, but she didn't know why. Nor would she allow herself to care.

The platforms rose quickly, pulling them through the chilled night air up to her waiting ship. A crewman grabbed her upstretched arm and hauled her onto the deck. The others followed. Within a few minutes, everyone was secured.

Sirens still rang out below in the city, and it wouldn't be long before guards flooded the harbor. Time to depart.

"Bastille?"

"Yes, Captain." He stepped up beside her, his towering, six foot four frame casting a long shadow on the wood beneath their feet, his bald head gleaming in the moonlight. "Release anchor and get us out to sea immediately."

She tucked her thumbs in the waistband of her pants, watching as the ship came to life. Harv and Mel, her technicians, raced to the engine room to stoke the electric tentacles of the Tesla engine. A couple of hands wound the cranks to release and raise the anchor. Steam bellowed forth from the exhaust ports. Her helmsman saluted, waiting for her approval to move the *Liberté* out.

Sorella nodded, and away they went.

As the ship moved away from the docking port and out over the open Atlantic, Sorella turned, ready to face her new passengers.

Both hunter and bounty stood between two guards as bald and tall as her second and trained to remove any threat to their captain, the crew or the *Liberté* on command. Soldiers befit with enormous benefits, including their own cabins and larger meal portions. Ultimately, they didn't need to protect her, but, according to her second, "Pirate captains always have protection."

"My name is Captain Castoa. Welcome to my ship." She opened her arms, sweeping them in a wide arc. "There are only two rules. One, you do as I say. Two, you break rule one, and your life is forfeit."

The crew members chuckled at that, everyone except her first mate and his guards. Laughs from them weren't common, and smiles proved to be far rarer.

"Happy to follow your rules, Captain. As long as you take me where you promised," the hunter replied with a smile of his own, a captivating one revealing less than perfect teeth, but a far cry better than Tuul's mangled mouth. For a man constantly facing danger, he seemed to take a carefree approach to his conversations and mannerisms.

"Name the location of *The Cursed*, and we'll be off."

A few crewmen stepped back then. She waited for him to announce the hiding place, eager to hear the name spoken aloud, for that was the secret to the gang's success—no one could find them. For years, they'd evaded not only the Germans, but the English, the Chinese, and the Americans as well. All nations longed to bring them down and coveted *The Cursed's* ability to get jobs done when they couldn't. Her father hated them with a passion, her mother whimpered at the mere mention of their name, and Sorella—she burned with vengeful desire.

The hunter stepped forward, closer to her, mumbling between clenched teeth. "I don't have an exact location."

"What the hell are you talking about? You retrieved a bounty for them."

He pursed his lips. "Yes, about that…. I did, but—"

She grabbed him by the collar. "Then where are they?"

Her eyes were so blue and perfect, despite her growling expression, that for a minute, Ian almost forgot the bargain he'd struck—almost forgot everything. Then he shook his head, clearing the momentary insanity away. He needed to focus if he was to keep himself alive, so he fixed his gaze on her lips, a pink, plump pair that had him licking his own. Noise ceased; everything went dead quiet. Then she scowled.

"Now, ma'am"—always start with a polite salutation—"the location changes frequently, as you know."

She let go and stepped back, hands reaching for a small piece attached to her belt. "Then what good is that bounty to me? Might as well kill him."

The captain moved forward, and he jumped in front of his bounty, putting his hands up, palms out and pleading. "Wait! I'm all for slaying bad men unless the act prevents me from getting paid."

"How about I pay you for the privilege of killing him?" she asked while her crew chuckled. Everyone wanted to see bloodshed.

"Normally, I'd take you up on the offer, but he's worth more than whatever francs you could give. I'll hold good on my promise to get us to them and split half of my reward, but can we get him locked up first?"

Tuul was leaning against the ship's side, and, with every passing moment, Ian wondered if he'd drop in to the water and escape. Not likely, since all the waters surrounding Europe were known for mines, especially close to shore. The damn things would send shrapnel shredding everything in its path within a kilometer if detonated. Sea travel was a damn thing of the past, thanks to Tesla and the kaiser.

She hesitated, looking at Tuul, then pointed. "Grab him." The two bald, dark-skinned guards hoisted him six inches in the air and headed toward a door under the helm's deck. "Take him to the hold. Then take our hunter to a room to bunk down."

"What about the choker?" Ian chose to ask the most innocuous question rather than one of the many contentious ones swamping his brain. Why did she want to meet *The Cursed* so bad? What was the metal piece she'd tucked back into the holster on her belt? With any luck, he'd be able to ask those questions later.

16

"Bastille will take care of it. He'll show you where to go." She pointed at the man who'd ridden the disc platform with her. "And, now, the directions you promised? Where to?" She motioned toward her helmsman.

"Northern Germany, old Denmark." Still looking at her, he held the controller out to Bastille, who towered over him by probably a couple of feet. "A town called Nordberg. Have you heard of it?"

"No, but that doesn't mean my crew hasn't." She walked away, back straight like a debutante at a ball. He was familiar with that type of woman. His damn heart had been broken in two by such a creature. A mystery to find in an airship captain the same form, the same swagger, as she mounted the steps toward her helmsman with grace and poise.

Bastille took the controller and motioned with his free hand. "Follow me," he said, his words a deep bass reverberating through the air and breaking Ian from his musings.

No sense in fighting the command or demanding more time with the captain. The choice to stay on the ship beat his alternatives. He'd need all his wiles to navigate the precarious situation he'd landed in. His constant string of bad luck would have his hometown's natives claiming he had bad juju, but then he'd survived worse. So far, his gut had delivered decent results, and he decided to trust the organ one more time. "Lead the way."

His escort opened the ornate wood door the guards had disappeared behind earlier.

"Mind showing me where my bounty is being housed?"

The question received a nod and a grunt, and they marched down a dimly lit, narrow metal hallway. While he hadn't been on many airships in the past, he found it odd that this one had wood planks trimming the wall edges then additional planks at certain intervals running from ceiling to floor as supports instead of the steel rivets normally used. The electric bulbs illuminating their way hung from the ceiling and were nearly the same size as a human head. At full strength, they'd burn skin, but they had been dialed down, giving off a hazy yellow glow.

Ian and Bastille walked past several doors; one he swore went to the kitchen, based on the smells drifting through the air. His stomach grumbled. It'd been hours since he'd wasted the few francs he'd had left on a poor man's bean stew and a slice of crusty old bread.

They passed three more doors, each labeled with a different ship's function, everything from the sick bay to the chart room, until finally they reached one with *Brig* carved into the wood.

Bastille opened it and stepped inside. "He'll stay in here."

Ian peered into the room, noticing the steel cage with electrified bars first. Very similar to the setup he'd busted Tuul out of a mere hour before. "Are you sure he can't get out?"

"You think you're funny locking me up in here." The man in question looked up, then, from his seat on the cell cot. "I'll be having the last laugh, you bloody bruisers. And when I get out, expect some payback."

"*Oui*," Bastille replied, his French accent thicker than before as he motioned for Ian to move so he could exit. "He'll be given two meals a day unless he misbehaves. Then the *con* will get shocked instead." *Idiot* in French was one way to describe Tuul.

Leaving the brig, they continued walking down the hallway. More gateways appeared, this time with numbers on them.

"These are the cabins," the first mate announced, stopping before a wooden entrance marked with a seven. "This one is yours."

Ian grasped the handle this time and pushed. The timber door swung open, and he stepped into a dark space. No electric bulb on in here, only a circular stream of moonlight coming in through a small porthole in the far wall. He let his eyes adjust. The tiny room was furnished only with a cot, slightly larger than Tuul's, and a small table next to it.

Feeling along the wall, he found the switch and flipped it. A small spark, the faint smell of burnt hair that accompanied a light coming on, and then the room illuminated. He saw the small heating unit and walked over to it. A sharp sting hit his fingertips as they briefly brushed the block.

He rubbed his hands together to chase the sensation away. "Does this keep the room heated at all times?"

"*Oui.* As long as the engine is on, the heating units work."

"Good." *Because where we are going it'll be colder than Spain.* "That captain…. She's got a princess air to her, eh?"

Bastille cocked his head and narrowed his eyes.

"No disrespect, of course." Ian walked away from the heating block and moved toward the bed. "I just thought she acted like many debutantes I know." He was rambling on, fishing for information on a sexy, angry captain he didn't even know.

And he soon discovered that was a bad idea.

He turned and found his companion looming over him. "You'll stay away from her."

Those were the last words he heard before a brown fist, the size of a brick, hit him square in the chin.

Chapter Two

Ian woke with a massive headache. After checking his clothes and weapons, he found everything in working order. Now to check his face.

Sunlight streamed through the porthole. He had slept several hours since Bastille dropped him, and someone had brought him a bowl, pitcher, and washcloth, setting it in a nice, neat grouping on the small table.

He reached inside his coat, feeling for the private pocket where he kept a special watch with a small mirror in the top part. The silver piece had been his grandfather's and displayed a raised image of the country manor his family owned on the shores of Lake Pontchartrain, a home he'd never be welcome in again. The thought left a sour taste in his mouth.

He flipped open the fob, balanced it in the palm of his hand, and checked for cuts or open wounds. Infections were dangerous; disease ran rampant and unchecked everywhere because medical supplies were closely monitored and doctors were only available to the rich. While he believed his host to be generous and maybe even a bit genteel in some respects, he doubted she'd spare limited antiseptic and bandages for an unofficial crew member.

Thankfully, he had no open cuts, only a bruise on the underside of his jaw. A cheap shot, one he should've seen coming, and undeserved in his opinion. He tucked the keepsake back in his pocket and gave himself a brief wipe down with a damp cloth.

Cool and pleasant against his skin, the cloth left behind the illusion of clean. In the skies or on the ground, you were never truly clean, at least not in Europe. So Ian settled.

Settling involved water, most likely cycled through multiple uses, on a semi-clean rag. There were visible stains from previous use, but the fabric smelled like lavender. Scents of such caliber were expensive and unlikely to be found in anyone's possession, especially on an airship

Cleaning ritual complete, his stomach growled. Locating food struck the top of his list. He headed in the direction of what he'd believe to be the kitchen the night before. Sure enough, his instinct was spot on.

He walked into a room where a woman in a pink ankle-length dress, white cap, and white apron bustled around a large stove. She whistled a tune he vaguely recalled from the ballrooms he'd visited years ago, though what grabbed his attention most were the smells of coffee and biscuits permeating the air.

"Good morning, ma'am."

The cheerful woman turned and smiled. "*Ciao, bello.*" Hello, handsome. He recognized the words only because his mother's housekeeper had spoken the language fluently. Picking up a few phrases had happened naturally over the years.

He nodded in acknowledgement and gestured to the coffeepot on the stove.

"Ah, *si. Si,*" she said, grabbing a cup from an open cupboard and pouring a steady stream of dark brown liquid into it.

He extended his hands to take it from her, but she refused to hand it over until a dollop of cream and a sprinkle of spice were applied. As he finally embraced the chipped porcelain, he blew over the top, watching the cream melt into the coffee.

The woman smiled at him and pointed at herself, "*Bonita. Te?*" You.

"Ian." He brought the chipped porcelain to his lips and tilted to receive the gift inside.

Instead he got burned, the hot liquid splashing against his lips as a hand gripped his shoulder, hard.

He hissed. "What in the Holy Mary?"

Bonita crossed herself at his words and reached out, taking the mug, which he gladly relinquished.

He turned and found himself face to face with Bastille. "You want a go at round two?"

The man raised an eyebrow. "No, but the captain wishes to speak to you in her quarters."

The fact he had gotten an invitation probably pissed the first mate off, but after ruining his morning caffeine indulgence, he didn't care.

"All right, lead on."

His guide turned and exited the room. Before he could follow, the lovely cook, her auburn hair peeking out the sides of her cap, handed him another steaming cup and a roll.

He smiled and inclined his head as his mama had always taught him. "Thank you kindly, *bella*."

A few quick steps helped him catch up to Bastille, who was already down the hall and knocking on the door across from his. The entire night she'd been footsteps away, a temptation for sure. He'd always been a sucker for beautiful women, and it'd pay to remember that now.

She called out, "Enter."

Ian followed the gargantuan man as they walked into a room with colorful silk cloths hanging from a bed, draped over tables, and serving as curtains around a much larger porthole. The adornments and wood-carved vanity against the far wall gave the room an exotic texture, suggesting he'd been transported to a harem in East India. He'd never seen one, but whenever he imagined a harem, it looked something like this, only with more women.

"Good morning, ma'am." He offered a standard greeting, something neutral, as he stepped into her lair. The captain stood behind a desk, focused on the maps and lists she'd laid out before her. She was scribbling notes and looking ten times the dish she'd been the night before.

Her gaze came up from the papers, and she didn't spare him a glance. "Leave us, Bastille. Alert me once we arrive in Nordberg."

"Aye, Captain." The first mate departed, shutting the door behind him.

"Alone at last." Ian took a sip from his coffee cup and a bite of the roll, enjoying the delicious combination of the sweetness of the pastry and the bitter, blessed taste of roasted beans. "How do you get coffee on this ship? I haven't had it in months."

"I smuggle it as good sky pirates do. Now what are we going to find in this town?"

He held up a spare pinky and motioned to his mouth. *Mama's first rule: never talk with your mouth full, especially in front of a lady.*

24

He took those masticating moments to get lost in her face, her deep blue eyes, the lines of her eyebrows—midnight black like her hair. Except for the bang line hanging over her forehead, the bulk of her tresses hung in two long braids, flowing past her hips like twin ropes. He hadn't noticed any of this the night before. No, her beauty had been tucked up and hidden underneath her head covering.

"Nordberg," he paused to clear his throat, "is where I'm to meet my contact. They promised to leave a man there to meet up with me and tell me where to drop the bounty."

He chose to leave out the part about where he'd been expected a week prior. No sense in causing worry. Sometimes the rules of survival trumped Mama's rule about honesty being key.

She put the pen down on the desk. "Where should my men look for him?"

"I thought I'd take care of that."

"I'm afraid your leaving the ship is out of the question." She shrugged. "I don't trust bounty hunters, especially ones who are working for the most cutthroat mercenary gang in the world."

He finished the last drop of coffee and set the cup on her desk. Sadly, it hadn't lasted long enough, much like her illusion about who he was. "I'm not a bounty hunter."

"Really? Then what are you?"

"A merchant coerced into bounty hunting. My name is Ian Marshall, at your service." No sense in denying his true profession. By N'awlins standards, he qualified as a merchant, an illegal one, but still....

"That explains a lot of things, but I'll still have to

insist you stay on the ship and let my men retrieve your contact. I don't trust any man willing to do *The Cursed's* dirty work." She stepped around the desk that separated them.

His breath hitched as he glimpsed her wide-legged trousers and belt, all of tanned hide, paired with a matching leather vest over a white blouse. Rubber soled boots completed the ensemble. Something about a woman in clothes intended for a man awoke a few anatomical parts he'd rather leave sleeping. His experience with women came from ballrooms and gatherings where ladies preferred fancy dresses with long trains and exposed backs and wore cloying perfume designed to choke the life from a man.

He shook his head. "Bad idea. My contact is supposed to speak with me. He won't talk to anyone else."

"Oh, we're not going to talk. We're going to bring him to you. Then you can ask him where his boss, Luther, is hiding." She stopped less than a foot away and leaned back, resting her palms on the desk.

"I thought this was a conversation. You state what you want, I state what I want, and we compromise, as God intended."

The comment earned him a flash of her priceless smile. "If God believed conversation led to compromise, then the kaiser would've never started a war."

"I'm not talking about the past; I'm speaking about the future." The attraction and want winding though his limbs demanded he take a step forward, a step closer.

"You seem to forget that, like Germany, on my

26

ship there is only one rule."

Maybe he imagined it, but her breathing sounded shallow. Did his presence affect her the way she affected him?

"A good leader knows when to break those rules." He leaned in, catching a hint of gardenias surrounding her. "You smell—"

"We've reached Nordberg, Captain," Bastille announced as he shoved the door open. No censure in the first mate's voice, just matter-of-fact truth.

The captain side-stepped him and pivoted, putting necessary distance between them. Thank goodness because he'd been ready to do something he'd probably regret.

She turned, the playful look from earlier gone. "Where is the contact?"

"He'll be at the Boar's Horns tavern; no names are given. Say to the barkeep, 'I seek one who's lost all hope.'"

"Anything else?"

"The contact will respond with 'You'll not find him here.'"

***

Two hours later….

They'd anchored in port, and Bastille set off with one additional guard to retrieve the contact. Yet Sorella still thought about the near kiss the merchant-bounty hunter had attempted. No use even thinking his name or making things personal, except she'd been ready to allow him the opportunity to kiss her. How many men wanted such a thing? How many weren't threatened by her heritage or skills?

"Castoa, they've returned," said one of her hands from the deck railing

She briskly took the staircase from the helm area to the main deck, the tension in her shoulders melting with each step. This contact presented her with an opportunity to finally locate her target. If things didn't work out, she'd kill a *Cursed* pirate and a merchant who should've stayed home.

The deck filled up with crew members ready to watch like people attending the theater. So little entertainment in their lives. Ian had been summoned as well and leaned against the staircase railing. "Why Captain Chaste? Is that really your name?"

The fact he'd deciphered the definition of the Italian word *castoa* to mean chaste surprised her more than the fact he'd become the first one to question her chosen moniker. So far, this man had proved to be unlike any she'd ever met, and against all her instincts, all her training, a tiny piece of her normally indifferent heart prayed he'd survive.

"Are you sure this man will know the location?"

He straightened and tugged at the ends on his brocade vest. He guarded himself well, keeping all his belongings on him. The girl she'd sent to clean his rooms reported he'd left nothing to search. "He's supposed to. I can't say he'll talk with an audience."

"Well, he doesn't have much of a choice."

"Aye, aye, Captain." He stepped away from his post next to the stairs and toward the edge of the ship, expression shuttered. She'd effectively shut down personal involvement. Then why did guilt gnaw at her gut like rats with scraps?

Instead of being allowed to arrive in a dignified fashion, *The Cursed* contact was tossed onto the *Liberté* deck like a sack of potatoes. His hair was long, his face unshaven, and his ratty brown clothes hung from his frame. The doomed soul looked every bit as disreputable as regular street trash.

"Are you sure this is him?" she asked.

Hauling himself over the deck edge, Bastille rubbed a hand over his bald top. "The *con* responded to the summons that he," a thick finger pointed toward Ian, gave."

The idiot now stood and plucked at the shoulders on his long coat, putting it back in place. "You'll set me back on the ground if you know what's good for you."

Sorella walked toward him, crossing her arms and slipping her hand up to the balisong holster underneath her jacket, the cold metal against her skin a reassurance and a temptation. "I don't believe that's an option right now, Mr…?"

"Heim."

"Indeed. First, I don't negotiate with known killers and people who generally steal from anyone to make a profit. Second, I have a gentleman on my ship who wishes to speak with you." She stepped to her left, giving way for the merchant-bounty hunter to come forward. Her crew, men who'd lost family members to the slave trades and clandestine practices of *The Cursed*, closed in on three sides. He wouldn't escape here alive regardless of the information he possessed. There'd be no way she'd be able to grant his passage. She'd promised those of her men who had suffered at the gang's hands a chance to kill any gang member, given the opportunity, if she didn't kill him first. Ian had survived merely because he'd claimed to be a bounty hunter, freelance.

The hunter spoke next. "Where is the rendezvous?"

"Why would I tell you now? You welched on the original agreement."

Ian glanced at her with a frown. He'd warned her against this, but she couldn't risk him bringing trouble to her ship or anyone taking Tuul by force. If that happened, she'd never have her chance to find Luther.

"I can't deliver the goods if I don't know where to go." The charm this would-be bounty hunter employed fascinated her. He grinned and cajoled where she'd maim.

"There's others that will be only too happy to take the bounty off your hands." Heim smiled. "I'll make sure to let them know where you are."

To hell with patience and difficult people! Grasping her balisong, Sorella moved quickly, bobbing around the merchant's body. A flick of her wrist, and the blade flipped open. She stabbed, sure and true, right into Heim's chest then pulled back. A reverse pull closed the blade, and she secured it in her holster as the unfortunate man fell.

"I'm afraid the bounty isn't fair game," Sorella replied, motioning to her men to finish the job. They swarmed. The contact had turned out to be a dead end. Time to start reviewing the maps again.

Not bothering to spare a glance toward her companions or the dead body, she strode down the hall, heading for her cabin. Boot steps sounded behind her, heavy and ominous. *Here's where the merchant will wear out his welcome.*

"Why did you kill the one person who'd tell us where *The Cursed* are hiding?"

She reached her door and stopped. "He wasn't going to tell us anything."

"You don't know that. I could've worn him down."

Such a statement required a laugh. "Really? With words or false promises?"

"One. Both. Why does it matter as long as you get the answers you want?" He'd moved closer, filling her personal space with broad shoulders and a clear view of the stubble forming on his chin.

"Yes, it does. I don't deal in false promises or threats. I deal in action. Word spreads, and then no one doubts my level of patience. No one hesitates to answer questions."

She knew Bastille stood a few meters away, waiting for a sign or motion to remove a threat from her presence. Leaning back she called out, "Tell the boys to pick the body clean, all belongings removed, wrap him, and store him."

"Aye, Captain."

Then she strode through her cabin door and slammed it in the merchant's face. *He can think what he wants, ideals and such be damned.* She'd been robbed of a part of her family and had deployed all her talents and skills to locate the person she'd lost. A dealer in coin and goods couldn't understand that, and explaining was a waste of precious time. Her lack of explanation and clipped words were the best deterrent she had, short of killing the fool.

31

Hopefully, he'd be afraid.

Chapter Three

Ian stared at the wood door for a minute, confused as hell. He still didn't fully comprehend how the captain had done it, how she'd killed a man in less than five seconds with one move and without direct contact with her hands. Anger superseded all else then. The woman apparently thought killing solved every problem. At this rate, he wouldn't gain his freedom at all.

Heim's words echoed in his mind, too. Others were happy to finish the job, meaning that since Ian had failed to deliver his bounty a week prior, Luther had already spread the word about Tuul.

Damn. He pounded the wall next to the door. Only one option remained. It'd mean going to his hometown and entering a skin trader's den. No sense letting the captain continue to control this situation. He knew more about *The Cursed*, possessed more knowledge about their contacts and allies scattered across continents, than anyone on this ship.

With a mind to put her in her place, he opened the door and walked right in. When he turned to shut it, giving them privacy, a steel whistle rent the air, followed by a loud thud. To his left, a metal blade, its two handles locked together with a small clasp, protruded from the wood inches from his head.

He rotated, eyebrows raised.

"Who gave you permission to enter?" she growled at him. Why the sound of her deep voice went straight to his groin, he didn't know, but the attraction rose regardless. Even the knife in the door, the idea she could murder without hesitation, but didn't, made him want her. *Damn it to hell.*

"No one but you needs to know where to go next, and I have that information." He stepped away from the blade, walking further into the room. She'd taken off her jacket and stood, white blouse visible, bosom obscured by the vest, at the far side of her cabin. He was starting to pay attention to body parts he shouldn't. "What the hell did you throw at me?"

Confusion bloomed on her face, and her brows furrowed. "What?"

"The knife. What is that thing?"

"A balisong. Why?" She stood on the other side of the room still, near the porthole.

He stepped up to her desk, looking at the map pile. "I like to know what people are trying to kill me with."

He failed to hear her move, didn't even know she'd taken a position behind him, until he felt a sharp edge slip through his shirt seams and poke his belly.

"If I wanted to kill you, you'd be dead."

"Why don't you?" The words came out in a whisper. Somehow, her close proximity called for such a thing.

She removed the knife and slinked away to stand on the opposite side of the desk. "Because you said you can tell me where we go next. Who would know where they are?"

He shook his head, clearing away the sexual want she'd left in her wake, and began flipping through the maps on the table. She didn't interrupt him but stood quiet and vigilant as he searched for what he needed—the map of the United States of America.

Finally, he found it and pulled the parchment from the bottom of the pile to the top. "When's the last time you crossed the Atlantic?"

"Six months. Maybe more," she replied, leaning in to observe where he was pointing on the map. "New Or-leans?" Her pronunciation was slow, but accurate.

"Yes, that's where we have to go."

"Who's there?"

A cutthroat asshole who'd sell anyone if given the chance. "A man. Janken. He's a jazz musician."

"And a slave trader." She'd heard of him.

"Didn't you hear? The United States abhors the slave trade. They don't deal in it." He let the sarcasm come out thick.

"Lies told by a president bent on pretending his country is pure."

It'd been twenty years since Wilson had closed the United States borders to Europe and other countries, ten years since the now serving President Franklin D. Roosevelt had been elected, and five years since he had acknowledged limited trade and held discussions with the kaiser. Those talks had centered around potential partnerships between a German-ruled Europe and a self-sufficient United States, a country home to citizens who sold the children they couldn't feed and searched black markets for items only found overseas.

"So you're for the kaiser then?"

She shook her head. "Never. I despise politics and prefer to steer clear. Better to stay in the skies and be free."

"You call this freedom?" He looked around the

room. Sure, her personal touches were there, but they didn't make the cabin feel like home to him. "This is a place to hide."

Walking over to the door, she dislodged the balisong. "You may call it that, but, as for me, I've never been more content."

Turning, she angled her hand, the movement subtle, but strong enough to send one of the balisong handles flying, the blade dancing in the air. Half a second later, the blade was still, cradled and secure between the two handle pieces.

His jaw dropped at her precision with a weapon so small, but so deadly. It reminded him of her. He snapped his mouth shut as she raised her head and speared him with those perceptive eyes.

He met her stare, saying, "If we leave immediately, we can get there in two days."

"Two? More like three." Her skepticism surprised him.

"I thought this ship was fast."

She laughed. "It is, but you need wind to get there, too. Even if I had all the power in the world, the breeze is at a standstill. Unless we catch a current, which is entirely possible once we get over the Atlantic—"

A clanging bell from the upper deck echoed through the ship. Bastille burst through the cabin door. "Captain, a German Inspection Patrol has hailed us and is preparing to board."

Great. He looked at Castoa, trying to gauge her reaction. She slipped her jacket back on and secured her balisong in its sheath. "Secure Tuul and keep him quiet. I'll handle the inspection." She grabbed a small

36

satchel of papers and stormed from the room.

"Follow me," Bastille said, and Ian had no choice but to trail along. If Luther desired Tuul, no doubt the German authorities wanted him, too.

***

The inspectors had already boarded by the time she got to the main deck. One man harassed her helmsman, waving an electo wand around and demanding papers.

"Herr Inspector," she called out, extending her leather pouch with all the documentation about *Liberté* and her ownership. If anyone looked closely, they'd know the papers were fake like her name and the clothes she wore. Still, she resisted the urge to fidget or tug on the scarf she used to wrap her braids. The martial arts trainers had beaten those inclinations out of her years ago. She'd faced more difficult challenges, from slogging through a mud-filled pit with all manner of deadly things to practicing with her knives until the cuts on her hands rivaled the indentations on her practice board.

"I'm called Dietrich. *Frau* Castoa?" Her name came out butchered and chopped like a pig at the slaughter. The inspector rifled through the papers, not even casting a glance in her direction.

"*Ja.*"

"Do you know anything about a man called Herr Heim?"

I killed him thirty minutes ago. "I'm not familiar with the name."

"No?" Dietrich looked up from the papers, his

37

beady eyes locked on hers. His bushy blonde mustache twitched as he spoke. "Then why was he spotted boarding your ship?"

The bartender probably reported them. The body rested below decks, being disfigured as quickly and quietly as possible.

"I'm not sure, though we did speak with a man about a job. Didn't catch his name, but he went on his way not long ago."

"Indeed. Did he say where he was headed?"

Sorella shook her head. "No, he did not."

"And you didn't think to familiarize yourself with a man with whom you might do business?"

"Not when his business isn't going to be profitable for me and mine."

Two other inspectors charged through the door under the helm's deck to search the cabins and every other nook and cranny. The kaiser's men told as many lies as anyone else. The truth was rare these days, and everyone, at one time or another, possessed the moniker of thief.

"Are we likely to find any undocumented cargo aboard?" A high eyebrow accompanied the question.

She shrugged. "Like I mentioned, we've been searching for work. There's no cargo beyond our own belongings and food to feed my crew."

Minutes ticked by as they waited. The unspoken rule when inspectors boarded airships was that the captain had to stay on the upper ship deck with the lead inspector until the official search or seizure was completed. A captain's attempt to leave the deck implied guilt, and then the men took twice as long searching. Usually, they'd claim a ship was carrying black market goods even if no evidence existed then seize the ship along with the crew, sending them to who knew where.

Sorella and her crew had heard whispers of work camps where men and women labored on various projects—making weapons or digging tunnels—but she refused to put weight behind such thoughts. Instead, she maintained a cool, calm demeanor through deep breathing while the search went on although she turned her back once and hastily crossed herself. Even bad Catholics still prayed in moments of dire distress, and this counted as one.

Forever and a day seemed to pass until both men returned to the top deck along with Bastille, who stood behind them. They exchanged their findings with Dietrich, a few whispered remarks, no items were presented, and then the inspector spoke.

"There's a man in your brig. Your crewmen in the room said he'd been put there for insubordination. Yet this man and another in the brig do not meet your original crew count listed here." He waved the papers at her.

If this turned bad, they'd slit throats and make a quick getaway. Nordberg would join the list of towns to avoid in the future.

Hopefully, these men were easily convinced. "That's because they're new recruits. Joined my crew less than a day ago. We hightailed it here for a job, and I haven't had a chance to update the paperwork."

The inspector glanced at the other crewmen on deck, sweeping, hauling, and scrubbing through their work. He wouldn't bother corroborating her statement because everyone on board would agree with the captain or face hunger. Food proved a precious commodity on land. On a ship, food was guaranteed to all who worked for it.

He eyed her again, taking in all of her this time, head to toe. "The man in the brig already caused trouble?"

"You should know yourself that townspeople, drunkards, and drifters aren't familiar with the strenuous work aboard a ship. They tend to believe it'll be as it once was for them."

"*Ja.*" He nodded. "All's good, then, except my men noticed your meat is not hanging but lying flat. I'd recommend you hoist everything off the floor, or it could spoil. You don't want to risk running out of food. Update your paperwork at an airship station as soon as possible. Others are not inclined to be so lenient."

"*Danke*, Herr Dietrich." The native Deutsch rolled off her tongue instead of the spit she'd love to hurl at his boots. Thankfully, the inspectors had believed Heim's body to be food and not disposal. Pure luck. Somehow the *Liberté* still had some.

The German departure lifted the mood immediately, as if everyone on board had been holding their breath the entire time.

"Where's Ian?" She'd keep her momentary weakness, the small part of her that worried about the merchant being hauled away, to herself.

"He's in the brig with Tuul."

"That's a bit dangerous." Sorella headed for the lower deck.

"I don't think so, Captain. When the inspectors asked, I'm afraid I didn't have a good reason for the

40

extra men. The bounty hunter came up with the same reasoning you did. Like twin minds." Bastille followed her, their brisk march getting them to the brig in record time.

She stayed silent. Her first mate's defense of a man she wanted to kill and at the same time embrace was disconcerting. Slamming the door open, she entered to find Ian leaning against the far wall, one foot propped up against the steel and wood beam behind him.

"Are they gone?"

"Would you believe me if I said no?" Wait, had she really said that? A glance at Bastille and his downturned lips told her she'd been flirting. Not captain-like behavior, and not like her. The merchant seemed to expect it though. He approached her in measured steps, slow and deliberate like the metronome used to help her control her speed when she was in training.

"I'd say you're trying to spook me."

Her skin went hot. Maybe this was something akin to blushing or, worse, maybe she'd contracted a fever. His words made her feel like the woman she'd been before the escape, before she'd left home in search of her brother and *The Cursed*. She'd been trained to navigate the upper echelons of societies, to live among royals. It'd be a lie to say she didn't miss the flirtations, the banter, and the niceties of her former life.

"I know better ways to scare you." Targeting her anger at him, she found the courage to look this man in the eye, to push past the sliver of desire he'd awakened in her.

"How?" His question hung provocatively, a whisper in the air. He stood less than six inches from her. Before he could blink his eyes, she'd reached for a balisong, opened it, and placed the knife tip near his groin. He gulped. "That'll do it." It'd be a lie to say she didn't enjoy having this man at her mercy.

She turned to Bastille, keeping the knife in position. "Let the helmsman know we sail for New Orleans immediately. The map to the city is on my desktop for reference."

"Aye, Captain. What about Heim?"

"We'll ditch the body once we're over the open Atlantic. Let the sharks have him."

The first mate nodded and left to execute her orders. No questions, just action. Why couldn't this man under her blade do the same?

She pulled back slowly, watching Ian's facial expression as the hint of fear in his eyes was replaced with confidence as soon as she tucked the balisong in its sheath. He liked to appear tougher than he truly was. She respected his approach.

"You will provide my helmsman with information about the location you intend to take us to. When we arrive, I will accompany you."

Ian shook his head. "I don't think that's a good idea."

"Why not?"

"Because you're too quick to kill people. Doing something drastic to any Howl at the Moon club member of Janken's will get your whole crew murdered before we leave port."

His lack of confidence in her crew wounded her a bit. As for her penchant for killing, she wouldn't deny enjoying the feel of her blades sinking into flesh, the feel of steel punching through the first layer of skin and finding purchase in an organ or a piece of tough muscle. Even imagining it brought goose bumps to her arms. Especially when those who were on the receiving end were part of the gang who'd kidnapped her brother, or anyone who wanted to harm innocents.

"How about I promise to wait until your signal to kill someone?" He also didn't know who she truly was.

"How about I go with Bastille?"

She raised an eyebrow. "No, you'll be going with me. I won't discuss the matter further."

"Fine, then," he growled.

Having awakened from his nap on the brig cot, Tuul laughed like a hyena. "Looks like someone doesn't like it when the bloody she-bitch cuts him off by the balls with little more than words. Let me out, toffer, and I'll put her in the right place for you."

She ignored him. He'd get his soon enough.

But Ian motioned for her to follow him into the hall, and she did, out of sheer curiosity. Once away from Tuul's view, he smiled, a bright smile that lit up his green eyes and made him seem younger. "I'll take you with me, but only if you agree to a wager."

"I don't wager."

"Not even for the opportunity of a lifetime?" He winked.

This man had to possess female admirers in every port as mercenary he was with his charms and fair looks. "All right, what's the wager?"

"If you take a life in New Orleans, you have to kiss me."

"Why on earth would you want that?"

He laughed then, the full-bodied laugh, so different from their captive's. One that spoke of someone familiar with happy memories. "You kill people with small knives, escape jail cells, captain a ship, and are smaller than any person manning such a ship. Who wouldn't want to say they've gotten a kiss from you?"

The blush stole into her cheeks again. She had deliberately kept her face dirty, her hair bundled up so no one would know or admire its length, and still this man seemed to want her. As an assassin, she should say no, keep the control in her favor, but the girl inside, the one who grew up too soon, wanted this one moment of fun, this one chance to experience a game, a lark. She'd beat him, of course.

She thrust her hand out. "It's a bet."

Chapter Four

Three days passed with little excitement. Ian found himself settling into life aboard ship; the ebb and flow of the crew working to keep the vessel moving and in good repair, the lighthearted banter among crew members, Bonita's hearty meals prepared with few ingredients and tons of flavor, and the little to no presence of a certain captain beyond her recurring role in his nightly dreams. In those dreams, her long braids were unbound, hair fanned out across his bed as she begged for his touch.

When he'd awakened this morning, he'd had no choice but to take himself in hand and relieve the tension. It'd been a long time since the mere thought of a woman had brought him to such a state. The fact that he'd failed to control his desire made him long for New Orleans. He was even a bit eager for the dreaded conversation with Janken in the hopes she'd fail to control her bloodlust, and he'd win the bet. He truly was a sick man, willing to sacrifice a life for a chance at getting a kiss. How far the landowner's son had fallen.

Now he stood on deck, waiting for the clouds to clear away as the *Liberté* began its descent into his hometown. He'd spent his childhood on the shores of Lake Pontchartrain and his early teens making a name for his merchant wares in the French Quarter streets. His ability to get black market goods, items unavailable anywhere else, from *The Cursed* had made him infamous and positioned him to hit the major markets…until the day he'd been figuratively stabbed in the back by the one woman who'd promised to support him in all things.

"My cook says you're from here." As she took a spot next to him at the ship's bow, the captain's maddening gardenia scent gave her away before her words were uttered.

"You speak Italian."

"*Si, signore*." She gave a half bow and a hand flourish for good measure. "I was born in Italy. Bonita also speaks English."

He stared. "You're joking." The woman had interacted with him every morning and spoken little or not at all. Any words she had shared were in Italian, and he had only understood half of them.

"I'm not."

He scoffed. "Well, at least she understands every word I say."

"She likes you."

The captain's covered arm brushed against his coat. For a second, he wished they were two people meeting on the street. He'd take her to Café Du Monde for beignets and a café au lait treat, But they weren't ordinary people.

The clouds cleared then, and the blue lake appeared, distinct against the surrounding swamps. The city seemed smaller, but he caught a glimpse of transport barges starting the trek up the Mississippi. Fishing and transport boats dotted the bay like grains of rice.

"I've talked with Bastille, and I'm familiar with the location you've outlined. How should we portray ourselves?"

Again the captain's question startled him out of memories, some bittersweet and others too precious to forget. "I'm known throughout the city, but will have to go by another name. Merely refer to me as Merchant if you must call me something."

"Are you marked?"

"Yes, I'm wanted by the New Orleans authority. I've been identified as a threat to American Normalcy." Such a label was given to any person who engaged in black market trade, skin trading, or the sinful ways of Europe.

"Ha. You're not dangerous."

"To be marked in this country doesn't mean you have to be dangerous. You only have to do something they don't like."

"What did you do?"

"Trusted a woman." Ian longed to take back the bitter words as soon as they left his mouth. Yet, he spoke truth.

Surprisingly, the captain didn't seem offended. "You're not the first fool to be taken in by a woman, and you won't be the last. What else do I need to know?"

Sorella turned the conversation, hoping to quash her flash of jealousy and her desire for revenge against the woman who'd hurt Ian. How easy it was to get caught up in the stiff set of his shoulders or the narrowing eyes honing in on the city that had spurned him. Her crew and purpose required that her emotions be disengaged like a good assassin. Yet he'd quickly become a part of her crew, the people she'd sworn to protect. He'd ingratiated himself with Bonita, the technicians, who were always searching for new jokes, and even Bastille, who seemed to enjoy his fun-loving nature.

"The best way to interact with Janken is to remain silent, and, if you can, cover those teeth. If he sees those perfect teeth, we'll be fighting every person on his payroll. I want to win my bet fair and square, not by baiting."

She'd forgotten about flashing her smile. She showed it rarely and only on occasions when she had some incentive. "I'll black them out."

"Good. Though Janken's not a bad musician, jazz is his secondary profession. First and foremost, Janken is a hardcore skin trader. He will also want to trade for information. We have to give him something good. Do you have any information to trade?"

A million thoughts flitted through her head. Locations of safe houses scattered throughout Europe. Names of those in the kaiser's inner circles, but not advertised openly. She finally settled on the one piece of information that would benefit anyone in a black market and secret trading business. "I do."

"Well?" Ian motioned with his hands as if to say "tell me."

She shook her head. "No dice. I'll share the information only once and only to Janken." This knowledge didn't need to be spread from ear to ear. Most people would laugh and call it a rumor, but to speak her true name would cost a lot. "Anything else?"

He glanced at her and let out a sigh. "This guy is a bit of a shock when you first see him. Rumors are he looks strange because he made a deal with the devil in exchange for becoming a musical prodigy. He doesn't see like you and I see, either. Don't think that makes him weak. He's not. The best way to deal with him is to be impassive. No fear, no surprise, and definitely no anger."

"I'm perfectly capable of that." She'd trained for years with martial arts masters, thieves, and cutthroats culled from the vast supply the kaiser had gained through the war. They'd come to her, trained her, and left once she'd mastered each task. The first lesson she'd learned was how to remain unaffected by her interactions with people. How to disarm them—physically—had quickly followed.

"You say that, but are you prepared for what you'll see? Prepared to not take action?" Ian's eyebrows rose.

"I've stood this far from a killer of millions and kept myself from spilling his blood. A skin trader who's not like other men will be more an annoyance than a threat to my temper." She'd pay penance for any evil thoughts later, and hateful inner musings required far fewer Hail Marys than murder did.

He rolled his eyes. "You say that now, but when we arrive at the club, I'm sure you'll think differently."

"If he's so awful, why isn't he marked?" To be openly disgraceful surely incurred wrath from the American government. Her own culture embraced diverse relationships, even sinful ones. As with all horrible things, as long as the proper penance was paid to God, they'd be forgiven.

He laughed then, loud and unashamed. The sound filled her ears, and she failed to stop the smile his open humor brought to her lips. Only when he abruptly stopped laughing did she realize he had found her ignorance surprising.

"One thing about N'awlins you need to learn…. Superstition will stay even the heartiest American patriot. The culture here is home to Voodoo and provides enough kings, queens, curses, hexes, and supposed witchcraft to leave a mark on anyone born here. Janken uses this superstition to his advantage, and the authorities won't touch him for fear he'll bring some evil to their families."

She'd heard of similar things among her own people, the superstitions Italians held about the mountains in the northern part of the country, rumors about bands of thieves and gypsies who'd gut families in their sleep…. Such fears kept travel to main roads, limited exploration, at least by peasants, and incurred the condemnation of the Church.

"I understand, and I'll keep that in mind." She left him then, disturbed by his admissions and how they inspired thoughts of her own homeland, a country she planned on never seeing again.

***

Sending Bastille and his men out for supplies, Sorella took the afternoon to relax and, eventually, to nap. Performing the meditation and focusing techniques taught to her over the years, she willed the bundling nerves winding their way through her body to release their tension.

To lie to herself and say her body's stress came from her situation and not from a certain merchant benefited no one. Instead, she embraced her desire and accepted the truth of her situation—Ian inspired a latent excitement, an emotion she'd only experienced through killing. Betting for kisses, dangerous liaisons through the New Orleans streets, and the allure of Voodoo. Such things hadn't existed when she was being trained to kill, then bred for social perfection, and, later, thrust into the role of group leader, which had required her to be responsible, not frivolous.

Now she followed Ian through the French Quarter. People milled everywhere, drinks in hand, cigar smoke curling above the throng. Hawkers sold their wares, from children to weapons, whatever was needed. Slowly dipping toward the horizon, the sun still shone, but its illumination was lost among the tall buildings and low alleys.

For this trip, she'd donned her typical boots, pants, and vest, but had added her duster—a leather concoction traded to them by an American who had hailed from the far West. He'd recommended it to her as a way to keep her body shielded from dirt, rain, and any other elements. So far, it'd been worth the electo wand trade.

After what seemed like an hour of walking through the streets, they came to the center of the square. Edison's fancy bulbs served as street lamps in these parts, Tesla's hard work having been shunned as un-American. He'd been out of the United States' favor from the moment he'd allied himself with the kaiser and begun creating weapons.

A park loomed in the center of the square, a safe place in which thieves could hide and jump out to rob unsuspecting passersby. Best to steer clear of that area if she wanted to win the bet.

Yet what really caught her attention was the cathedral, enormous and rising from the earth like a symbol of purity. Clear cut, white marble, its steeples reached toward the heavens. *To attend mass in such a place.*

"It's beautiful, isn't it?" Ian whispered in her ear.

"*Si,*" she murmured and then realized she'd stopped in the middle of the cobbled street to stare at this monument to the Almighty. The heat from the man at her back seeped through her coat, setting a blaze through her.

"We're headed right over there." He slid an arm around her shoulder and pointed to a well-lit building on the far corner. Tesla coils burning on the corners wound around one another, forming a large sign. The purple electricity continuously spiraled through the coils, announcing to the world that those inside did indeed "Howl at the Moon." They appeared impervious to God and the government, set up across from a church and using technology banned in the United States.

Ian took a step forward, motioning at her to leave the peaceful serenity the church invoked for the harsh, cruel, and depraved environment of the club where Janken ruled. If that weren't enough, the women and men lining the pavement in front of *Howl at the Moon* made her stomach turn. These were the scum who sold their children. Clients needed only a few coins to use a child for an hour; a few more coins were required for permanent purchase. The parents didn't care who bought their offspring. The money meant food, rotgut whiskey, and illegal drugs, all to

dull their senses or appease the growl of their bellies.
He'd been right. She wasn't ready for this.

Chapter Five

Ian glanced back, hoping the captain was keeping a hold on her nerves. She'd appeared so confident earlier, so sure of herself. If looks were capable of murder, he'd no doubt all the sellers lining the outer walls of the club would be dead.

He stepped up to the glass doors and stopped, waiting until she stood beside him. "Whatever you've seen out here, it's worse beyond the club's threshold."

The frown on her face deepened.

"You can't let it affect you. If you do, they won't talk to us, and we'll be in the fight of our lives within five minutes. Follow me." No sense in even double checking her expression at that point. If she failed to get rid of her scowl or appeared to pass judgment on the disgusting acts taking place at every table, they'd be ejected or attacked in minutes.

The majordomo came from between twin red velvet curtains hanging from the ceiling, the only barrier between the innocuous lobby area and the sin beyond. Ian heard the jazz, though. The mournful sound of Delta blues, a sad, wailing cry as if the city itself were in pain, infected every cell.

"We're here to see Janken," he announced without artifice, opening his jacket to show his lack of weapons. The sharpest item he carried was a pen knife in his boot for picking locks if a quick escape became necessary.

"What about her?" The broad shouldered, burly man pointed an uncharacteristically short, knobby finger at the captain.

She appeared bored, but opened the sides of her coat. Her electo wand hung from her belt, the balisong she'd thrown at him before out of sight.

The majordomo turned his hand palm up and grunted at her, "The wand, here."

Relinquishing the weapon came with no outburst, no fight. The only thing she said was, "Can we go now?" coupled with a yawn. A woman bored or, at the very least, disinterested.

"Janken is playing now, but he'll see you when he's through. Sit at the first table to the left of him." Instructions given, the majordomo swept the velvet curtain to the side and allowed them to pass.

Ian motioned her to move in front of him. He wanted to gauge her reaction, and, surprisingly, she didn't even glance at the couples embracing around her. At least one partner at each table was a child, some in their teenage years and some younger. All manner of depraved men and women accompanied them, wanting everything from conversation to more. Booths lined the walls, and tables were scattered throughout the room. The balcony up top housed the private suites with drop curtains which offered discretion to those who'd rather their transgressions be confidential. Everything was trimmed in either white or blood red, the two colors so often used to symbolize purity and sin.

When they reached their assigned table, Sorella paused, focusing on the swaying head of Janken, his white, shoulder-length hair moving with the music as he attacked the strings of his guitar with long, pointed fingernails. "The better to pluck with," Ian remembered him sharing once upon an evening, years ago. Sorella seemed mesmerized, caught in the twangs and vibrations of the melody. She appeared to have locked onto the same things he had.

"Would you like to sit?" he whispered and pulled out a chair. He enjoyed the little shiver that started at her shoulders before reverberating through the rest of her body.

She glanced at him, then the chair, and sat down without a verbal response. He moved into the seat next to her and looked back to their host.

The crooner had finished his song and was brushing his hair out of his face with one thin hand. Pale and pasty, his skin held little pigment. His eyes, too, seemed devoid of color, resembling snow more than anything else. People called him the King of White; some even claimed he was the offspring of the Voodoo Queen of New Orleans and a Danish prince.

"*Merci, mon petites.*" The albino's voice sounded like gravel in the cylinder-shaped microphone. "I'll be breaking for a short time. Youse keep yourselves amused and stay out of trouble."

"Remember…let me do most of the talking," Ian said as soon as the crooner stood and started making his way to the edge of the stage.

The captain merely nodded, taking in the other members of the band, who didn't leave their spots on the stage.

Instead, they started playing again, a perky jazz tune with a good measure of saxophone. A few of the couples positioned around the room came out to the dancing square and began swaying or grinding to the beat. Ian kept his expression neutral although his gut churned at the visual.

Their host grunted as he pulled back a chair, and, as a guest, Ian stood, as manners dictated. The captain didn't.

"Standing on ceremony as if you were still a gentleman?" Janken chuckled.

Ian sat and smiled. "Mama's rules ne'er do disappear."

"Mine did, thank God." The albino tapped his long fingernails on the table top in perfect rhythm with the beat from the stage. "Who's your friend? She smells like a garden."

"Castoa—"

"Captain Castoa of the *Liberté*." She'd cut him off and extended a hand in peace.

For a blind man, Janken saw remarkable things, and he grabbed her, leaning forward over the small table. He flipped her palm between both of his and sniffed at her wrist. Without rebuke, she submitted to his eccentricities while Ian experienced a sudden desire to throw the skin trader from his seat and put the captain's fancy knife through him.

"Divine. Absolutely delicious." Then he let her go. "Such a pretty scent for a woman around filth and dirt all the time."

They all fell silent. Ian couldn't find his words at the moment, a red haze of jealousy winding its course through him. Being jealous of a blind man seemed a bit ridiculous, but at the same time he wanted permission to touch her, to smell her—liberties denied him that Janken had taken without even bothering to ask..

Luckily, he didn't have to produce the next piece

of conversation; the albino did the work for him. "Now what does a marked want so bad he's willing to darken my establishment with his sinful presence?"

Time for business. "I need to find Luther."

"You're not the only one."

"I've got merchandise he's requested, but a delay had me late to our meeting point. I know you can tell me where he's hiding." He'd bet his life on it.

The two illegal-dealing men weren't friends, but information about anything and everything black market or top secret seemed to be in the albino's possession. *The Cursed* were always in need of intelligence. Information allowed them to stay one step ahead of the authorities and determine who'd want their services.

"I may know something, but the rules still apply."

Ian nodded. "Yes, and she's got something good to share."

A white eyebrow rose. "Eh? What could this marvelous woman who captains an airship full of foul-smelling, disgusting men have to tell me that would equal such a trade?"

Her time was up. Sorella didn't want to dole out the one secret keeping her safe, but she'd run out of choices. "Merchant, leave us."

"Are you sure?" Again, a concerned tone, as if he worried for her safety. More likely, he feared for his own as men in her world were want to do.

She nodded. The fewer people who knew, the better. Yet once she had shared it, Janken would no doubt auction her secret to the highest bidder.

Ian rose from the chair and stepped over to the

stage, keeping his back to them. The distance and the music reduced the chances he'd hear something he shouldn't.

"Come, *ma fille*. Tell me your secret."

She took a deep breath and slowly exhaled. How long since she'd said her real name out loud? "My name is not Captain Castoa. It's Sorella Corvino."

"*La farce.*" He laughed, loud. The gravel in his throat rattled, giving away the extent of his smoking habit.

As if to prove her point, he pulled a cigarette case from his jacket and offered her a smoke. Sorella shook her head in polite refusal. He shrugged and went about lighting one for himself. "You don't laugh, so I must believe it, then. Fair Princess, our soon-to-be-queen, they search for you everywhere. Papers run charming articles about your self-imposed religious studies, fooling the American public, and claim you won't wed the president's son until you've completed them. The truth is, you've marked yourself. Why?"

"I don't wish to marry."

"*Non*, a beauty like you deserves to be loved. You know I'm part French; my mother told me the greatest thing we can give one another is love, especially of the flesh, the ability to feel pleasure. Hence, I encourage it here."

She kept silent because, to her, this place represented forced, sold, and disgusting recreation. Children were being exploited in every corner of the room. Screw the bet. If she could take every sick adult in the place out without retribution on her crew, she'd do it. No matter if it meant hours in prayer as

59

payment. Yet, Ian had warned her their host already knew the *Liberté's* port number and berth as he kept apprised of all ships porting in New Orleans.

"The type of pleasure I like, my fiancé wouldn't support." Especially since she'd been tasked to kill him and his father.

"Ah, I knew some sort of twisted fetish drove you. I sensed such a thing."

Another moment during which she opted for silence, even though she wanted to say things to make his balls shrivel rather than placate his ego.

"Ian." A pale hand waved in the air. "Come back over and join us."

The merchant did as instructed, and a nervous brick took up residence in her stomach. Did their blind musician have loose lips? Not possible if he wanted to remain in business.

"Her information is good." Janken took a drag from his cigarette and blew out rings of smoke directly at her, taunting her. "And quite valuable."

"So you'll trade?" Ian sounded a bit eager, his eyes wide as he glanced first at her then at the skin trader. Selfish bastard.

Janken nodded and licked his lips. "I will, but only if *le capitaine* confesses her favorite guilty pleasure."

So he wanted a demonstration. She'd half a mind to cut his throat. It'd be quick and messy, but….

Then she heard the scream. More like a wail. Turning in her chair and ignoring Ian's senseless tapping on her arm, she glimpsed a hunched wall of a man. Standing taller than six feet, he was dragging a girl toward his lap. The toothless grin, paunchy belly, and soot-colored clothes gave away his poor status.

Today he'd been paid a small wage and had decided to spend it on a child, the most affordable being this small waif with waist-length ash-blond hair, a threadbare dress, and a face filled with fear as she struggled against her villain's arms.

The child's pleas of "no" and "stop" were answered with a slap to the face, knocking her to the floor.

"Let me show you pleasure," Sorella said to Janken, shrugging Ian's hand away from her. In the course of ten steps, she reached the struggling pair. The ugly molester had risen from his seat and was leaning over his prey. Sorella slipped a balisong from the hidden holster inside her vest, flipped it, and plunged the blade into the bastard's arm pit, a quick jab and release followed with additional stabs to both kidneys and, finally, his stomach.

He only got a chance to groan "What?" before stumbling to his knees.

Sorella grabbed the little girl under her arms and dragged her away just as the giant pervert fell, face first, onto the floor, dead. "Are you all right?" she asked.

Eyes wide, the waif's gaze darted between her attacker and her savior. Then she nodded.

Only then did she notice the men surrounding them. Not club participants, but men dressed identical to the majordomo, the same ones she'd glimpsed hiding in the shadows of the room.

"Leave the females be, and remove the body," Janken called out.

She took the opportunity to move the girl to the side. "What's your name?"

"Gretchen."

"All right, Gretchen." She began steering the small thing toward her table. "I'm going to have you sit in a chair right here." They stopped at a table two away from where her host and partner watched them. "Don't leave. Don't move. Because, when I come back, I'm going to get you out of here."

"Really?" Gretchen shivered, wrapping her arms around herself. "Why?"

"Because no one should go through something they don't want to, and, if you go back home now, it will happen again, won't it?"

Gretchen nodded. Of course, trading your children for money seemed a common practice here and in many other cities across the world. Kids were no longer prized for their innocence; they were valued for the services they could deliver, most usually for the use of their flesh.

She helped the girl get comfortable in a white metal chair with the same plush red cushions that adorned all the seats in the room. Then she returned to the table where Janken and Ian still sat. "There is my pleasure. Bringing weak, disgusting men to their end."

Janken smiled. "The rumors are true, then. Beauty has been trained to kill, not merely to act as a decoration on a man's arm. But do you protect the one you marry or take orders from someone else? That's the question."

He'd receive no hints from her. Her secret was now forfeit to him to use however he wanted, which might easily lead those looking for her right to her ship's starboard side. She refused to give him anything more.

Ian cleared his throat, frowning. *"The Cursed?"*

"Ah, yes. You'll have to speak with Mistress Eva. At the moment, I believe she's the only one who'd know." Janken tucked his cigarette case back into his pocket.

"I thought Luther was done with her."

Their host chuckled, a low, raspy rumble. "Never believe every rumor you hear. If anything, Luther spread the whispers himself to keep suspicion away from her. He didn't need anyone threatening his dish. The man has enough to worry about, *non*?"

The news didn't leave a smile on her partner's face. In fact, his furrowed brow and scowl said something else entirely, something the albino, in his blind glory, recognized.

"Mon ami, I never promised the sun and stars. This is all I know." He rose from the chair and leaned against the back of it. "I must ask you both to leave now. Your presence, and especially that of our lovely client killer, is bad for business."

Ian shoved his chair back and stood, glancing at her. "Are we taking the girl?"

"Yes."

"Then let's go."

Sorella was used to giving the orders; in any other situation, she'd knock him down a peg. Yet a wild look had entered his countenance, coupled with a silent frustration. Mistress Eva was obviously someone he didn't want to see.

She stood, ready to call the girl to her, when Janken called out, "Oh, others have already asked me about your package. If they have information to trade,

I will gladly share your direction." *So much for secrecy.*

Gretchen's hand tucked in Sorella's, the trio left the building without speaking a word or exchanging a glance. Once outside and away from the wall of people still looking for buyers for their children's innocence, Sorella slowed and asked, "Is there anything you need, Gretchen? Do you want to say good-bye to your family?"

The little one shivered. "No, they'd only want you to pay them. Are you a princess?"

White lies were better than truths sometimes. "I'm a captain."

Chapter Six

Once they reached the ship, Sorella turned the girl over to Bonita's care. The cook knew plenty about young charges, having been a keeper of girls not so long ago.

Sorella moved to confer with Bastille, but not before Ian growled, "I can't believe you'd be so reckless."

"Excuse me?"

"Your little stunt in the club. Killing a patron? We're lucky Janken didn't have us skinned alive as an example."

Sorella took a deep breath. "Is it me you're really angry with or someone else?"

"You. Risking our entire operation because of a girl." His shoulders hunched, he looked downright livid. His brows were furrowed in a never-ending scowl.

"Maybe you've forgotten, but the albino wanted to know what my guilty pleasure is. I had no choice. Thankfully, I got to execute such a task on a rapist."

He ran his hands through his hair, tugging on the ends. "But why keep the girl?"

"Why not? Her family doesn't care about her. If they did, she wouldn't have been inside that awful club." Time to level with him. He'd spent plenty of time telling her his tales of woe. "I know what it's like to be unloved, to be thought of as a possession rather than a thing. I watched the person closest to me, my brother, be ransomed off to *The Cursed* for my safety, treated like an object, and given up without a fight." She left out the parts about how her brother had protected her, sheltered her, and shown her emotions their parents never had. He'd been her first true family member. Since then, she'd come to call many others her family, but none of them was related to her by blood.

The merchant threw his head back, staring toward the sky. When he finally acknowledged her again, he said, "I understand, but that still doesn't mean I agree to it." Then, he marched off.

Ian stalked down the hall to his cabin and slammed the door behind him. *A waste of a trip going home, evading patrols, and praying no one recognized me.*

He flipped the switch and moved to take off his coat, but the swath of pink skirts and a heart shaped face surrounded in mahogany curls stopped him.

"What are you doing here, Dixie?"

She stood, flashing an all-too-familiar smile meant to charm and placate. "The first mate let me on when I told him I needed to talk to you."

"Who did you say you were?"

"Your sister." *No shame.* The woman had never displayed any in the all the years he'd known her, from the moment they'd met until the moment she'd betrayed him.

"Thank goodness I don't have a sister, or any siblings for that matter. Now, get on with it."

The less time she spent aboard, the better. Too bad his porthole was too small to shove a female in three layers of skirts through.

With a flutter of her hands, she brushed the curls

from her face, angling her chin so he'd catch a good look at her black-and-blue eye. Fresh from the previous night's argument, no doubt. "Your cousin's a madman, Ian."

"Ah, so you've discovered how he likes to deal with situations he doesn't agree with."

"I made a mistake."

One of many, in his opinion. Yet, his ability to change anything had ended the day she'd confessed his activities. "You spun your web. I can't help it if a bigger spider took up residence."

She pouted. "There has to be something you can do. Someone you know. All those illegal contacts…. You're familiar with people who can get rid of him."

Funny how, over a year prior, she'd been singing a different song, one involving the authorities and a promise from his cousin to keep the family name clear of the problems tainted un-American activities caused.

"Are you ready to pay the favors those types of requests cost?"

"What favors?"

He enjoyed how confused she sounded, how the concept that such dealings didn't come free escaped her. A lovely part of being the daughter of an influential landowner and never needing to work for the clothes on her back, or anything else for that matter.

Ian stepped forward and reluctantly put his hand on her shoulder so he could steer her toward the door. Then, a thought—"How did you know I was here?"

"I have some friends working for the docking port. Told them to keep an eye out for you."

It wouldn't be long now. "You know he's following you, right?"

"So what?"

No time to lose. He opened his cabin door, ready to shove her out and head for the helm. Instead, he nearly ran face first into the captain. Somehow he pulled up short and got a squeak from Dixie as he trod on her leather-clad toes.

"I heard you had a visitor?"

"Yes," he nodded. "And she's leaving. As are we."

"I thought I told you before. I give the orders on my ship." She stepped forward, crowding his space. He wished Dixie was anywhere but in this room because he wanted nothing more than to grab the woman in front of him and make her experience the hot lust her close proximity generated in him. Her words, demanding as they were, chased away his anger, replacing it with something much more dangerous.

"Yes, you did. I'm making an exception since the she-devil behind me has led my cousin and the police right to us."

Dixie poked her head around him. "Hi. Could you do me a favor and kill my husband?"

"I take it her husband is your cousin?" the captain asked with a smile.

Ian wanted to pull his hair out. "Yes, and he'll have the authorities on us faster than we think. I'm surprised they're not here already." He grabbed his ex-fiancée's arm this time. "You're off this ship immediately. No one is killing anyone."

"Unless you can pay for it," Castoa chimed in.

There was something off about the way she eyed

him. Not in anger, but amusement. She looked downright splendid standing there, leaning against the doorjamb, her hair still covered by the ridiculous headscarf. Meanwhile, a manipulative female, whom he'd once believed loved him, tugged at his grip on her arm while slapping her small hand purse against her bustled skirts with the other hand.

"Let me go. She said she'd do it if I could pay."

"In human parts." The captain whipped out her knife then, flipping it open and shut.

Dixie gasped. "Why, I never." Then, her struggling began in earnest. "Let me go. Now! I won't let someone mutilate my body. Foreigners, depraved people. Uncivilized Europeans. I'm leaving."

Ian released her as if she was a hot Tesla coil, and she ran, the heels of her shoes clicking on the floorboards until they faded away.

"I already paid off the police, at least for the moment. Until your cousin offers them more." The words rolled off her tongue matter-of-factly as if this sort of situation occurred every day. His pants tightened at her words. A woman who feared nothing, who didn't believe in danger.

"Very generous of you."

"Hmm?" She stopped playing with her balisong knife and looked at him.

He came toward her, arms open, expecting her to move away from the door and put distance between them. She didn't. "You protected me at your own expense."

"I thought you might take my generosity as replacement for me losing the bet."

Less than six inches separated their bodies. The pulse point at her neck fluttered, her breath shallow. Her knife stilled in her hand, closed, but ready to deploy. She waited for him to make a move.

The distinct possibility existed he'd be dead in the next minute, but her lips were deep red in the low light, like cherries he'd eaten in late summer. To leave them untouched would be a crime. "You thought wrong."

He leaned in. She gasped, and then he kissed her.

She'd been kissed before, but it had merely been her parents' chaste touches to her cheeks or forehead, and, once, her fiancé had brushed her lips with his. Otherwise, she had remained untouched until now. As he touched the tip of his tongue to her closed mouth, a sinful sensation swamped her body. Gooseflesh broke out underneath her clothes, and little hairs stood up on the back of her neck.

Sorella grabbed the lapels of his coat and opened her mouth. Something carnal took over, an instinct to engage his tongue in some primitive dance. If this was considered uncivilized, she'd gladly abandon society and all its norms.

As fast as the moment began, it ended, and Ian pulled back a few inches. "You taste amazing."

He did, too; like peppermint, and…. "You taste familiar." Not as if she'd tasted him before, but somehow the aromatic tang of his mouth and the scent of his breath on an exhale resonated within her. She'd bottle it if she knew how. "Kiss me again."

"As my captain commands."

The next meeting of their lips was frenzied, their

mouths battling for supremacy until she was drowning in everything Ian. He swamped her brain like the waterlogged forests of his homeland. As he pulled her flush against him, consuming her every rational thought, she felt the hard ridge of his arousal against her belly.

She moaned.

He moved them further into his cabin, slamming the door shut behind them. "Step back," he mumbled, breaking contact briefly.

She did as he commanded, not bothering to worry about losing control. She was more concerned that if she didn't follow his request, he'd stop this exquisite pleasure.

"Hands up above your head."

Another command; another one she'd follow. Only when her hands were in place did he begin pressing kisses to her jaw then chin and neck. His palms began to rove over her body, feeling upwards from her hips until he stopped at her breasts.

"Would you let me touch these without the clothes?"

She could hardly breathe or think. On the verge of saying yes, she remembered her uncertainty about giving this man such liberties. Until tonight, her body had been pure of all sexual interaction. Maybe her mind hadn't, but that held no significance.

Ian lifted his head then. "You're so beautiful, Cap—I really can't call you that when what we're doing is so much more than standard ship activities." The smirk on his face, the dimple forming above his eyebrow—those things made her forget. Made her revel in the innocence of their encounter. She adored the fact he had no idea who she was and wouldn't angle for a play even if he did. A first name wouldn't hurt.

"Call me Sorella."

"Sorella." Her name left his lips as a whisper, the sweet sound of a priest's prayer to *Dio.* It touched something in her, put a crack in the steel wall she'd erected against romantic emotions. "May I open your vest?"

She smiled then, unable to believe such a gentleman existed in their world of cutthroats, slavers, and the destitute. "More action, Merchant."

He inspired anarchy. She'd truly come to his room to find out where they needed to head next. Instead, she was standing against a cabin door, captivated by the way his fingers came up to the buttons on her vest and steadily worked one, two, three, and four of the casein plastic discs from their moorings. When that task was accomplished, he spread the sides of the leather apart and groaned.

She laughed. A shirt and silk camisole still separated his hands from her breasts. Yet as she looked at his face, he seemed enraptured by simply moving the original obstruction out of his way. "What are you...."

Her question trailed off when he leaned down and latched his tongue around the pointed tip of her nipple, apparent even through the barrier of her clothing. Without thinking, she dropped her hands onto his head, fingers running through his short hair, a pool of moisture in between her legs growing larger with every swipe of his tongue on that sensitive peak.

Finally she couldn't take anymore. "Stop." She

secured her palms around his head and pushed him away.

He appeared dazed for a moment, lost in lust. Then he slapped himself and cleared his throat. "Sorry about that. I got a little carried away."

She took that moment to secure her top and haul the gates shut on the desire coursing through her body. "Let's get back to business. Where to next?"

"Hamburg."

He had to be mistaken. "Excuse me?"

"Hamburg, Germany."

"You want to fly directly to the kaiser's homeland?"

Ian shrugged. "It's not like I'm saying we should go to his doorstep. We'll be hours away from Berlin, but yes."

"This Mistress Eva is there?" Crossing Germany's borders was a risky venture any day. With her three additional passengers on board, the risk rose exponentially. "If you can promise me this won't be another wild hunt without actual answers, we'll go. If not, you'll supply me with a second location."

He dragged his hands through his hair. "I can't promise you anything. Eva was—no, scratch that, *is*—Luther's woman. She'd told me things had changed months ago, but Janken has confirmed that's a lie. She'll know where he is. She has to. If she were in trouble, she'd need to be able to reach him immediately."

Silence ensued. Sorella's brain was still caught up in the memory of his kissing her mouth, kissing her breasts. She needed to flee before she asked him to do all those things again, to take this moment to even more dangerous levels of intimacy. Confession and meditation would take twice as long tonight.

"I'll tell the helm to change course for Hamburg."

"All right." His raised eyebrows and emerging smile made her self-conscious, and she didn't want him to see her as weak, to see her succumbing to his charms, so she opened the door and mumbled, "Good night," before slamming it behind her and heading for the top deck.

Trying to banish or at least defuse her recollections of a warm mouth, a willing tongue, and her desire-fueled heat, she focused on ensuring the *Liberté* left port before Ian's cousin got any ideas and making sure a certain frilly woman in pink had been expelled from her ship. She crossed herself as she walked, silently sending pleas for forgiveness to the heavens above for succumbing to the temptation of sinful lips and tender touches. Her inexperience with intimacy had been a telling thing. As much as she wanted to expel the memory of her encounter with Ian from her mind, she also desired to save it away for those lonely moments when she believed herself to be merely a tool and not someone worth true love or admiration. Ian's eyes had told a different story when he'd held her and fondled parts of her body never touched by another. Yet how fast would he turn her loose if given a chance at all of her? She couldn't risk it, not even for fond memories.

Chapter Seven

She avoided him well. Two days had passed since he'd kissed her, a mistake and blessing wrapped in one. Since then, his dreams had been erotic nightmares—his hands tracing the contours of her body, her breasts with dark nipples at the mercy of his tongue. Every morning, he awoke abruptly from his dreams, feeling as if some invisible entity, bent on preventing them from being together in the most intimate of ways, was shoving him away from her with some force.

On the third day, he searched the ship for her. Yet, every time he entered a room or deck, she'd left moments before to tend to another task, fix another problem. When he finally found her, she was sitting on a stool in the kitchen with a steaming glass of coffee in her hand, sharing a conversation in Italian with Bonita.

He didn't hear much except the words *amante* and *confidenza*, "lover" and "confidence," which hollowed his stomach and filled it with dread. He was treading new territory for a man who expected female betrayal. Most women he'd known were quick to abandon their men for a better deal or even momentary pleasure. His mother, his aunts, and many others had traded away their bodies, marriages, and so much more for personal gain. America was far from the land of the pure.

Sorella—in his mind, her name sounded like a prayer; a call to the angels above. *Damn.* He couldn't bring himself to believe she'd turn out like the other women in his life. Her untutored lips and gasps of surprise when he had latched onto her clothed nipple told him otherwise.

To keep jealousy from flaying his precarious sanity, he needed to change the conversation. Immediately. "Ah, two lovely ladies in the kitchen. A sight to bring any man to his knees."

Both ladies stopped talking and looked over at him. Bonita waved his statement away with her hand and went back to her rolling pin and the ball of dough on the opposite counter.

Sorella rose. "I have to get back to my cabin. I'm supposed to meet with Bastille shortly."

Before she could escape again, Ian moved to stand in front of her, palms out. "Wait one minute."

The glare she gave him had his cock rising to attention instead of withering away. "You'd be better off moving out of my way before I decide you don't need ten fingers."

He sighed. "Dirty words won't scare me off. We need to talk."

"About what?" A blush stole into her cheeks, a dead giveaway as to why she'd avoided him.

A tiny part of him wanted to bring up their stolen kisses in his cabin, but he thought better of it. The steaming cup of coffee and the multiple knives she always carried played a large part in his decision-making. "About Hamburg?"

"It's a city. You're meeting someone. She'll tell us where *The Cursed* are, and then we leave. Pretty straightforward."

If only things were half as simple. "No, I haven't

told you all the details."

With a roll of her eyes and two steps backward, she positioned herself on the stool once more. "I'll give you five minutes."

Time to talk fast. "Eva Sonne is the premier singer for the British Embassy. She performs three nights a week at special embassy events held in an attempt to woo the kaiser into a trade deal with Britain, one that will give the British a little more room to maneuver in France and Denmark. If we're going to pull this off, we'll need to be dressed in something much nicer than everyday clothes."

"You mean a formal dress for me and black and white for you?"

"That's the ticket. It will be polite conversation, no weapons, and plenty of nods and curtseys all night. These events attract the German royalty and British aristocracy quite frequently."

Sorella's face paled.

"Will that be all right?"

She didn't respond, but her grip loosened on her coffee mug.

Ian leaned in and nudged her with his shoulder. "Sor—Captain?"

His near use of her Christian name got Bonita's attention, and she bustled over to them, speaking rapid fire Italian and gripping the captain by her shoulders.

After a moment, Sorella shrugged off the woman's embrace, resituated her grip on the cup, and calmly replied, "I'm fine. I'm fine."

She then turned back to him. "It will be good. What else?"

Something about the idea of high society being present upset her. Getting her to talk about it with him seemed a lost cause. Instead, he mentally rambled through the potential pitfalls. So far, she'd shown proficiency in dealing with high pressure situations and strange environments. With the exception of her killing the rapist, she'd performed perfectly at Janken's club. He had only one thing left to ask. "When's the last time you danced?"

"What does that have to do with anything?"

Ian laughed. "At a party like this, dancing is the easiest way to move across the room."

"I'm afraid it's been a while since I strapped on those shoes."

"Then maybe we'd best practice before we arrive. If we want to avoid attention, we'll need to fit in."

She hesitated and took a long drink of her coffee. "Fine. Let's do it."

"Tonight?"

Sorella sighed. The cook nudged her again, which jarred her cup, spilling coffee over the side. "Tonight," she said, rising from the stool. "We're done here. I've got to meet Bastille and review inventory."

Then, of course, she ran off again. He didn't know the rules of this game, but his captain…he liked the sound of that…seemed on edge. It might make him a bastard, but he liked her demeanor when she was rattled, too.

***

First, the kiss. Then the opening of her vest. Now

78

the dancing. The man seemed to hunt for the chinks in her armor. Sure, the practice he had proposed benefited both of them, but such lessons, next to weapons and martial arts, were some of her favorite ones. Dancing opened the soul, allowing her to become one with the motions of nature, the very air around a person. She still recalled those short waltzes with her brother as her partner. Bodyguard, friend, and family were three of his many titles. The memories were imprinted in her mind, a symbol of his dedication to her.

She'd played off her knowledge about ballrooms and the activities of royalty, pretending to have no experience with any of those thing; the biggest lie ever told since she'd been bred for this exact purpose. Only a short time remained before she needed to appear for practice, and she opened the drawer of her vanity, tucking the red glass rosary inside. No doubt God laughed at her or chose to punish her for her sin. All her piety and prayer were not enough to atone.

Bonita swarmed into the room, a force of nature, her former lady's maid turned cook. When Sorella had chosen to run from her privileged life, her maid had insisted on going with her. One of the few privy to Sorella's secrets and loyal to the core, the woman had been with her since childhood. Like a second mother, a managing one, Bonita stayed close..

"*Ella-bella*, you must sit and let me put up your hair." She spoke Italian on the ship to keep their conversations private. Few people spoke the language, and Sorella worked hard to avoid adding nationals from her homeland to their crew.

She sat in the chair, and the old woman came up

behind her, brush in hand.

"We'll have to wash this mess, first thing, if you plan on going to the embassy tomorrow," Bonita clucked, unraveling the two long braids and brushing the waist-length hair out slowly.

"You're enjoying this."

The cook laughed. "Yes, I am. Who else is?"

"Ian and God."

"Watch your language. Taking the Lord's name in vain is the path to hell." The words were coupled with a brief smack to her arm. "Speaking of handsome devils, you told him your name?"

Sorella pretended to be deaf until the brush tugged her hair a little too hard, the start of a new, single braid. "Yes, I did. By accident."

"Is this the same accident that earned you a first kiss and a studious session with your rosary and bible?"

After the debacle two nights ago, she'd had to talk to someone. Since Bastille topped the 'out of the question' list, the only option stood behind her, yanking, folding, and twisting her hair to form a chain at the top of her head. Her nanny wanted her to take a lover, to cast aside the standards she'd held for so long.

"Yes, the incident is the root of everything." Including lingering sexual thoughts, which had caused her to touch herself the night before in longing, She had moaned in agony as release escaped her, another act of sin she'd paid penance for today.

"I still say if you want to make sure you're never forced to marry the horrible president's son, then you must remove all vestiges of their required purity.

Take Ian as a lover. His compliments are nice enough, and he looks at you like he wants to eat you." This last sentence came out with a giggle.

"It's wrong to fornicate before marriage." A pin poked her scalp, sharp enough to hurt, but she'd trained long and hard to avoid outbursts from small pains.

"Am I a sinful woman because I chose to allow men to worship this body when they respected and worshipped me?" The words were harsh and scolding.

"No, *Nana*."

"*Esattamente!* God wants us to be loved spiritually and physically. With the life you lead, waiting for marriage is too risky. Better to take a chance for a few moments of happiness now, especially when it's offered by a man that good looking."

Embarrassing, the whole thing. She still blushed at how she'd been so forward, allowing him access to more than her lips and nearly telling him to take her body, to claim it. If anyone had seen…. Saints be praised, no one had. So difficult to shed years of ingrained propriety.

"All done. Look in the mirror."

Sorella looked up, one solitary braid wrapped at the back of her head. "It looks very efficient. My hair won't fall in a fight."

The comment earned her a slap on the shoulder.

"No, this is just for tonight. Tomorrow, I'll make the braid shorter. After I wrap it up, I'll fold the longer pieces of hair underneath and pin it down to cover the braid. A unique hairstyle to hide the length."

She turned to the right then the left, imagining how

the final design would look. "Sounds perfect."

Bonita shook her head. "You don't even care as usual. No matter. Let's get you in the dress."

Launching out of her chair, Sorella turned and waved her hands. "No. Absolutely not. I'll wear a dress tomorrow. Not a moment before."

The woman ignored her and strode to the small closet on the far wall. Fleeing Italy, they'd packed serviceable clothes for her new life, but her maid had smuggled two fancy dresses out, in case of an emergency, she'd claimed. The Hamburg situation counted as an emergency, but why bring on the agony of remembering her old life any sooner?

"You have to practice in the dress and the shoes," her maid replied, turning around with a shimmery, cream silk confection of a dress, boasting a top with shoulder straps, a diamond patterned bodice, and a skirt capable of whispering over the floor with barely-there touches.

The shoes were cream colored as well with a small heel. No doubt she'd regret this, but Bonita looked so happy. It'd been a long time since the woman had had anything to celebrate besides successful smuggling operations and illegal activities concluded without detection.

"No sense arguing with you. Get the damn thing over here. I'm supposed to be up on deck in fifteen minutes.

"*Ella-Bella*, you'll be so gorgeous he won't be able to resist you."

The debutante living within her brightened at the prospect, even though trained assassins were only supposed to engage assigned marks. In this case, she was breaking all the rules.

Chapter Eight

Ian mingled on the top deck, waiting for his dance partner to appear. Dinner in the galley had been filled with conversation about music and entertainment. According to the engine techs, such things were scarce.

The full moon shone brightly, and Bastille's team kept the lighting to a minimum. Air warm, breeze light, the mood was set.

That's when she appeared. The light sounds of voices halted, and he turned to glimpse an angel. Her dress shimmered in the light with each step; his merchant eyes recognized silk by the way the moonlight reflected off the folds and bends of the fabric.

Her hair was pulled back, exposing her face and neck...a neck he remembered fondly. No sense thinking about things he couldn't act on.

His mother's lessons reared their ugly head. A gentleman never let his partner stand on the dance floor alone, so he strode toward her. Seven steps to get there, and he smiled. "You look gorgeous."

"Let's get this over with," she growled, extending her arms up as if waiting for him to connect with her.

"That's no way to avoid being noticed."

"Why would anyone notice us?"

He moved in then, and she gasped in surprise as he wrapped his right arm around her waist, clasping her right hand in his left. "Do you wear glasses? Your crew hasn't spoken a single word since you came

84

through the door. They're mesmerized. The same thing will happen at the party, and if you want to scare them away, death stares won't work."

Ian stretched out his hand, loving how he fit perfectly against her as the heat emanating from her body warmed his fingers. He inhaled and could smell her gardenia soap, fresh and strong. She'd cleaned up for this, and he hadn't bothered to dress up. Not that he could; he'd joined the ship with only the clothes on his back. His lack of proper attire rankled less than the idea that he probably carried a quarter inch of dirt and sweat on his skin.

No sense in wallowing. Back to business then. "The best way to combat the interest from the crowd is to be infatuated with your partner. The British and Germans are known for their marriages of convenience. If you play the role of besotted female, they'll never pay you a second glance."

Then he nodded at Bastille. The gramophone crackled as the record began to turn, and the sounds of the Blue Danube Waltz filled the air. "Do you know the waltz?"

"Doesn't everyone?" Until that moment, she'd been like a doll, silent and stiff in his arms. With those words her body relaxed, a different version of her coming to life.

"I'll lead." As he whisked her into the first turn, she glared at him. Drilled into him years ago, the steps played in his head. One, two, three, back and forth movements. She never trod on his toes like so many Southern belles had in the past. She didn't fight for control and gracefully flowed to the music, her skirt swishing along.

85

"Ready to move across the room?" he asked, eyebrow raised in challenge.

"I won't break if we do."

So move her, he did, in small, tight circles, then wide ones. Five minutes of twirling across the deck, passing Bastille, who waited for Ian's nod. Once he gave it, other couples joined them. Men with men, females with men. Enough to crowd the deck and give Sorella a sense of what a real ballroom would be like.

She tensed initially as their free space tightened. "How long is this song?"

"Ten minutes."

"Are all the songs this long?"

He laughed. "Not all of them. Are you already tired?"

"No, but these shoes will probably leave blisters on my feet. Curse Bonita and her need to play dress up."

More turns, more people whirling by them. He navigated them toward the center of the group and kept them there. He'd overlooked her increased height; only a few inches, but enough to raise the top of her head to the level of his nose. "Probably wise since you'll have to wear heeled shoes tomorrow night. Should we stop so I can check your feet?"

"No!" Then she attempted to take control and push them back into the circling group. "I can handle this. It's a pair of slippers, not a knife wound."

"You're trying to lead."

She gave him a predatory smile. "When a man won't complete the job, the only option is for a woman to take over."

86

"I like a female who knows how to take charge, but sometimes I think there's a point where it's good to yield."

The song stopped. Everyone clapped.

"Thanks for the practice." Sorella released her hold on him, but he didn't let go.

"One more dance."

"One more? What's the name of it?" She put her hand back on his shoulder and wrapped her fingers around his left one, fitting their palms together.

He nodded to the first mate. "It's a new dance. Not huge, but gaining momentum every day."

Another crackle as the record hummed to life, and then Fred Astaire's voice burst into song. " I'm in heaven."

Pulling Sorella closer, he let go of her hand and slid his own along her arm where he gripped the muscle right below her shoulder. Then he whispered in her ear. "This particular song requires you to get a lot closer."

They swayed back and forth as he fitted his cheek against hers. Her breath tickled the shell of his ear as she replied, "They permit this type of closeness?"

"In Europe, yes."

Her skin was soft to the touch, and her gardenia scent invaded his nostrils, ten times stronger than before. Sniffing her hair came as natural to him as moving his feet to sway with the music. The pulse point at the juncture of her chin and neck beat rapidly. His cock began to harden. Then her breasts came flush against him as they spun out of turn. Too much, too fast, and he nearly lost his footing. Next a dip, then a twirl away from him. The distance and fresh air cooled his heated flesh. *Damn.*

As he reeled her back in, she sighed. Their cheeks touched once more.

"A perfect dance for lovers."

The words were wrong, and she stepped on his toes purposely. Backing away from him, she mumbled thank you, turned, and ran.

He moved to follow, but Bastille and his twin body guards blocked his way.

The first mate eyed him suspiciously, announcing, "Dancing is over. Douse the lights, and back to your posts."

Ian wanted to take back the ill-timed lover comment. No, the comment spoke truth. He wanted Sorella as his bed partner, wanted a chance to hear the noises she made in the throes of passion even if only for a night.

"I'll escort you to your cabin," Bastille said beside him.

It seemed he and Sorella wouldn't be lovers tonight.

***

Sorella lay in bed, staring at the ceiling, restless. Yet she yawned, her vision blurry. Sleep wanted to take over if only her racing mind would let it. Unfortunately, her thoughts kept drifting to Ian. Remembering his hands on her waist as he glided her along the deck in the moonlight made her shiver anew. She'd barely stopped herself from doing the same thing in his arms.

Then that word…*lovers*…spoken with want and

prediction as if he believed it was only a matter of time until she'd let him into her bed. She'd run, desperate to keep her mental gates closed and her door barred, literally. Between the trunk up against it and the metal staff from her weapons cache as a makeshift bar, she'd erected a barrier, a visible line she refused to cross, no matter how tempting the proposition.

When he decided not to come after her, she was ashamed of her momentary hope that he'd not give up so easily. But men didn't fight for strong women; they bedded them to say they had conquered something unattainable. No, the best way to steer clear of disappointment was to stay away from men and keep all emotions in check. Foolish to think his interest in her was serious instead of merely a chance to make a boring journey exciting. Foolish, indeed.

Chapter Nine

A toss-and-turn night called for coffee. Ian also needed to get off the ship. The single horn announcing their arrival in Hamburg sounded a little after 5:00 a.m. according to his pocket watch. That meant he had a chance to get new clothes, a shave, a haircut, and all the things gentlemen of leisure pursued before a big event. Activities he'd been bred for.

But his first stop involved the kitchen. Then he'd find the gorgeous captain and get her seal of approval for his off-ship venture.

"*Bon giorno, Signora Bonita*," he called out as he walked through the small doorway.

Bonita dusted flour from her hands and wiped them on her apron. Instead of the shy smiles and blushes she normally granted him, this morning he received no acknowledgement, no eye contact. She treated him like an unwanted person, too lowly for notice.

"May I have a cup of coffee this morning?"

"No, *demone*," she spat at him with pure disgust. Demon.

A deep voice let out a laugh, and he noticed Bastille tucked into a corner, mug in hand, a small stool to support him.

"What have I done?" Obviously, he'd committed some sin in her book of proper etiquette to be called such a name.

"You play with my sweet Ella's emotions." Her

words were partnered with three jabs of a knife in the air in his direction. "She's no whore or some pretty girl to be mastered."

Ian snagged a chair from beside the smiling first mate and pulled it up to the prep table. The damned man was enjoying this too much. "I don't want to master her."

"No? Then why the games? Tell her straight.... That's right word?" She looked past him at Bastille. She nodded at whatever answer he provided. It wasn't a verbal one because Ian heard nothing. "Yes, tell her without games."

"I mean her no harm. If she wants more, she's welcome to it. I won't force her."

She clucked her tongue at him. "My Ella is special, *si*?"

He nodded. No use lying to anyone about that. The way the woman said the captain's nickname reminded him of the shy, reserved way Sorella had come onto the deck the night before as well as the precision with which she'd hurled a knife at him and scragged two men in the week he'd known her. Special, but deadly.

"You take her to this dance, no... erm, ball. It will make her vulnerable. Pretending to feel things for her when you don't will do the same."

He understood. Emotions were seen as a distraction and an obstacle to their work. Too bad his heart refused to listen to such things. If only he could will his desire to stop existing. Remove the engulfing urge to get as close as possible when she was near.

Bonita moved away, then, to the coffee pot, not giving him a chance to respond. Words failed him. How did he explain the passions Sorella awoke in him? Until he'd met her, he'd all but dismissed the possibility a woman existed who protected those she loved and believed in the sanctity of her relationships. Women like that were rarer than diamonds from America.

A loud creak rent the air as Bastille rose and walked over to him. "She's right. *Capitano* will need someone to watch her back in this den of wolves you're taking her to. You go somewhere we can't follow. Will you guard her with your life? Remove her if the situation becomes too much?"

Did they not know their leader? The woman handled people like carcasses. No doubt she'd carve up the whole room of royal attendees and guests with good reason. She equaled a hurricane battering against the Louisiana coastline. She'd ravage anything in her path, at least from what he'd glimpsed. "We are talking about the same woman, right? Your captain seems to be plenty capable of taking care of herself."

Bonita slid a mug of coffee in front of him. "This is different. Not like the other times when she's taking out a man who'd harm a little girl or some spy for that awful gang."

"What's different?"

Bastille chimed in this time. "It's not our secret to tell. Just swear you'll protect her."

An odd place to be put in, for sure, and he'd probably have a good laugh with Sorella over the whole ordeal later. Still, a good merchant never committed to something that left him in the dark and with no reward. Better to change the subject. "Were you and Sorella ever together?"

The old woman laughed and turned away from them.

The first mate's face twisted in disgust. "*Non*, that's like saying I'm in love with my little sister. Now before you leave tonight, you must meet with me. I'll give you a few things to take in with you."

"Scans and searches will be tight."

"These items won't be detected. A ring with smoke pellets and an EMP chain that will work as another piece of jewelry. If you don't know how to use them, ask the captain."

Ian gritted his teeth. "I know how to use smoke pellets and EMP chains. It's pretty ironic you're asking me to protect her when you don't think I'm capable."

A raised eyebrow and puffed chest were the physical responses in reaction to his offhand remark. For a moment, the possibility of fists flying amid male tension stood at an all-time high. Then Bastille said, "You're not a bounty hunter. You admitted that the first day."

Ah, the challenge. "Yes, but I've completed over half a dozen random missions for *The Cursed*, had guns pointed at me, knife wounds sewn up, and been around people ten times more likely than you to shoot me on sight."

"Have you killed a man?"

The only question that meant anything to anyone except Luther. In his travels, you were judged on the number of kills, not the number of missions completed without death, without injury. Nor were you judged on the ability to wheel and deal information like Satan trading souls for favors.

Ian took a long drink of his coffee, letting the partially sweet, partially bitter liquid sit on his tongue a moment before swallowing. "I prefer to conclude my jobs without death, to deal in sorrow instead." Then he locked eyes with Bastille to ensure his message was received. "But I've watched tons of men die by other's hands, and I can stomach seeing a man or woman's light extinguished."

The statement earned him a handshake. He took it, marveling at how his hand was so much smaller than his companion's.

"You'll do, Merchant. I'll see you later."

The pound of rocks sitting in his gut lightened as Bastille left the room. Ian went back to his coffee, and Bonita placed a roll in front of him.

"*Si*, you'll do." She leaned in, a small sliver of table separating them, and whisked out a paring knife an inch from his nose. "But if you break my Ella's heart…I'll cut yours out." She moved away immediately, not letting the threat linger. She didn't need to.

He chose that moment to leave the kitchen and enjoy the rest of his breakfast on the top deck while searching for Sorella. He hadn't agreed to protect her, but he'd do it simply for an excuse to be close to her.

***

Sorella tapped on the door and waited.

A small voice called out, "Come in."

Once she stepped inside, she left the door open, if only to give comfort. Closed doors usually meant privacy, but did not always guarantee you'd be left alone.

"You told Bonita you wanted to see me."

Gretchen sat on the edge of the bed, swinging her feet. In the few days since they'd brought her on board, she'd received new clothes, new shoes, and as many bowls of soup as the cook could get her to eat.

She stood up and curtsied. "I wanted to thank you for rescuing me."

"It wasn't a problem."

"I also want to ask you a question."

Sorella stepped further into the room, bending down on one knee so they were at eye level. "Anything."

"Are you a princess?" A pink blush stole into the child's cheeks as she spoke.

"Why? Do you think I am?"

"I heard a story about a girl who'd be a queen when she married, but she ran away instead. Her hair was like yours, and her eyes were really blue, too."

It didn't surprise her in the least. Stories passed along in the Americas were as bad as the tales told in Europe. She'd been to the States several times and had been introduced to dozens of people, members of Congress, world leaders, and many other dignitaries, as the future wife of the president's son. "Well, thank you, but I'm afraid I'm not a princess anymore."

"That's sad, but I think you're a great captain."

Sorella smiled. "Thank you. And what would you like to be one day?"

She expected to hear her say a princess or a fancy lady, as such was the way of young girls. Sorella's youth, outside of weapons training and deportment classes, had involved daydreams of fancy parties and being romanced. Soon, however, these had been replaced with the simple desire to do what she wanted when she wanted it. Too bad you need money for that. Instead of something fanciful, though, Gretchen leaned into her and whispered, "A cook."

"That's a very practical choice."

She nodded, her shy smile producing a little dimple above her mouth. "Yes, then I'd never be hungry."

"That's one way to look at it." A cook rarely went hungry, and in the world they lived in, good cooks were always needed to serve in some capacity. "How about we let Bonita train you?"

Gretchen stepped back, looking at the floor. "I'm not good at anything."

"Yes, but you're a member of this crew, and everyone in this crew works. Bonita has little to no help, so having you in the kitchen would make things easier."

"What if I make a mistake?" The question came out soft and filled with fear. Even her chin quivered.

"Then you'd learn from it." A captain knew the fear of mistakes. As a child, she'd been on the receiving end of canings and punches, nothing to leave permanent damage, but enough to remind her to avoid making errors in the future. Until his ransom, her brother had taken plenty of those himself for trying to shield her from punishment. "I don't beat or starve crew members. Here you either pull your weight, or get off the ship. You can go when you wish to. I refuse to keep people against their will or make them do something I wouldn't do myself."

Instead of speaking, Gretchen flung herself at

96

Sorella, wrapping her arms around her neck and squeezing her in a hug. Immobilized by the sweet gesture, she stayed in position, not mirroring the girl's actions, but being a post to inflict affection on.

When Gretchen finally pulled back, she wore a big smile and said, "Can I start now?"

"Yes, you can." She stood and moved out of the way as the girl started to move toward the door.

Seeing Ian standing in the doorway, they both froze.

"Don't mind me," he said, shifting to the side to let the girl pass.

Sorella wanted to ask if he'd heard the whole conversation, but found she didn't need to.

"Now you'll have to do what I ask, or I'll tell the whole crew the captain is a big drip, suckered in by children and handsome men."

"She's a little girl, and nothing like that lug I offed for you in Nordberg. What do you want?"

He stepped through the door, filling up the space and reminding her of how small the room really was. "If I recall, I never said I wanted you to off the guy." He set the coffee cup in his hand down on the small table near the door. "Since I finished my breakfast, I wanted to talk about getting off the ship to prepare for tonight."

"I have everything I need."

Shaking his head, he strode closer. Instinctively, she put a hand on the balisong holder at her waist, more to stop herself from reaching out than because she feared him. "You may have what you need, but if I show up in these clothes, they'll call the coppers."

She took in his worn jacket, his white shirt dirtied

by days of wear, his trousers in need of a wash, and his dusty brown boots. *Valid point.* "All right, that's fine. Anything else?"

"Your crew is worried about our meeting with the canary…eh, the singer. They want me to agree to protect you."

Of course, Bonita and Bastille would enlist him to watch over her. They'd avoided Germany for the last few years because the government wanted her back so badly. Her wedding was still scheduled to take place in six months. All she had to do was stay in hiding for that long; instead, the desire to find her brother had her doing dangerous things. "Did you agree?"

"No, I don't do anything unless something is in it for me."

Her fingers twitched, and she tapped her foot on the floor. *Damn men who didn't say what they meant.* "And what do you want?"

The question earned her a smile and the presence of his face less than six inches from hers. She wanted to kiss those lips, taste him again, and wondered if she'd taste the coffee he'd drunk earlier. "I want you and me alone in a room for one hour. I want you to tell me everything."

"Everything?"

"All the things you're not telling me. Why people are worried about this ball, why that little girl thinks you're a princess, and what you told Janken to get him to tell us about Luther and Eva."

"You're not asking a lot, are you?" she replied with as much sarcasm as she could muster. He was standing too close.

"No, I'm really not because I want other things,

too."

He dared her with those words and the twinkle in his eye. Dared her to ask what those other things were. She refused to give in. "I agree."

"With what I want or to wanting other things?" He was truly a master at manipulating words, no doubt a formidable merchant.

"I agree to tell you everything. My only condition—we won't leave until we have a location for *The Cursed*."

His turn to extend his hand. "It's a deal, and I'll even protect you, too."

Touching his palm to seal the agreement was a mistake. It cost her a shiver and revealed how much he affected her. Surprisingly, he didn't take advantage of the moment, no leaning in for a chaste kiss, no grazing her bosom, nothing more than a handshake and a release.

The fact he seemed unaffected by their momentary connection aggravated her. No sense in letting him have the upper hand. She unclasped her balisong and flipped it out, bringing the tip up under his chin. "When I want your protection, I'll ask for it."

She pushed him to the side and walked out. Let him wonder whether she wanted to kill him or not. She had things to do before tonight.

Chapter Ten

Hamburg, Germany

The afternoon had been well spent preparing for the ball. From a haircut to a fine suit, Ian had been lucky enough to have money from Bastille to pay for it all and still have a few *papiermarks* left to purchase a rose for his lapel. The first mate had promised to ensure a Teslauto would be reserved to take them to the embassy. The auto had arrived five minutes ago, but still no captain. His captain.

He stood on the *Liberté's* deck, tapping his foot. Fashionably late was one thing. Too late, and they might draw suspicion. Crew members were gathered on deck as well, no doubt to witness Sorella in all her evening finery. Even if she wore the dress from last night, she'd attract attention immediately.

He glanced out over the city, dotted in twinkling lights. Not far from the docks, he could hear the sounds of people out for the evening, though beggars and thieves roamed within their circles. From above looking down, the beauty of the landscape acted as a mirage against the true horrors remaining after the war. Injured soldiers discarded for youth and those who'd sacrifice without question. Women and children starving in turn, from lack of funds to pay for food after their own men were killed.

The scuffling and low conversations behind him died. She'd appeared. He turned and inhaled. A white satin dress with rhinestones clung to her figure; a mink stole covering her shoulders and hiding the dress's bodice. Her hair was a mix of shoulder length tresses at the back and short, rolled bangs at the front. With a little help, no doubt, from Bonita, she had transformed herself into a true princess. Where the hell she'd gotten the dress, he didn't know.

Men and women lined the deck, then, from technician to swabbie, each person bowing as she walked by with her guards flanking either side. When she reached Ian, she extended her gloved hand, and he held it in his own while bowing over it. If only they were different people…. He would wax poetic on her beauty and plan to hold her close until they returned home where he'd undress her. Instead, he hoped she didn't have a knife hidden somewhere and that they'd pull this off.

"Are you ready?" he asked, letting go of her satin covered palm.

"Yes." She snapped her fingers, and Bastille pulled the lever to start their descent. The rectangular platform they stood on was designed for cargo, but, in this case, it served as a lift to get them to the ground without ruining the train of his captain's dress spread out behind her.

Once on land and in the car, he turned to her. "You look gorgeous."

"Is this where I'm supposed to reply with a compliment?"

Ian smiled. "That would be proper."

She looked him over, taking her time to peruse his form from his shoes to his hair. "You're very dapper this evening." The words came with a flash of her perfect smile, something people would expect tonight.

"Wow. Even the smile is genuine. I do believe there's truth to the remark."

Sorella blushed. The auto moved them through the *St. Pauli* streets, the red-light district where airships ported, at a quick pace. Before long, they'd passed into the merchant district, *Sternschanze*, home to the expensive shops and townhomes of the wealthy, and not far from the City Centre where all political gatherings took place. Considering Hamburg the port to the entire world, the Germans allowed Britain and several other northern countries to open up embassies within the heart of the city.

Time to get things sorted. "When we arrive, I'll do the talking. Women are granted less authority, so let me lead."

"Funny how they think such a thing important." She spoke her musings with a soft, far-off voice as she looked out the window at the buildings passing them by.

"Such is the way of powerful men."

"Yes, but when you're outside of these trappings, power is wielded with weapons rather than words."

Nothing like a good ol' debate before dining and dancing. He couldn't resist. "Yes, but is it, really? These men are the gatekeepers like powerful men in most countries. Either through war or because of the nature of the world, they help determine with their words and decisions if you'll need to fight or yield your weapons to live."

She angled her head away from the outside view and narrowed her eyes at him. "Then we should just eradicate them."

"Never solves the problem. Someone else will always take their place." Ian had seen such things first hand when his father had slaughtered his uncle and taken over the family land. It wasn't long before he'd inherited and spent more time watching his back than managing his responsibilities.

"Then how do you live?"

"One day at a time, enjoying whatever happiness you make for yourself." Once he turned Tuul in for his freedom, his plan involved exactly that.

"What if killing makes me happy?" The question hinted at a challenge as if, somehow, her talents at blade-wielding made her less desirable. Too bad he wanted her more because of those skills, because of the sheer strength she possessed. The idea of merging their strength made his cock twitch. No sense in tempting the beast.

"If it does, then you should be given every opportunity to pursue it by killing men like that rapist you dispatched in New Orleans." He adjusted his shirt cuffs so they peeked out from the edge of his jacket sleeves, anything to get his mind away from thoughts of her lips and sliding across to her side to sup from them.

"You're a marvelous speaker, Ian. You could convince someone of anything."

If only her words rang true. "Unfortunately not. If that were the case, I'd be resting somewhere in the Caribbean or maybe running a small café in Budapest. I wouldn't be attempting to infiltrate the British Embassy of Hamburg to find out where an infamous gang of cutthroats is hiding so I can claim a bounty."

She didn't respond, but the bright, cheerful look on her face faded away as she returned to looking out the window at the passersby.

***

They exited the auto and approached the monstrous red brick manor house, which had been transformed into a location for parties and meetings concerning Britain and the German Empire. The line of Hamburgers attending trailed out the front entrance and onto the circular drive. Autos were dropping guests off at the street because of the crowd.

Sorella spent the idle minutes analyzing the outer structure of the mansion, the number of windows on the front and right side of the house, the height of the wrought-iron gate enclosing the property, and the number of stuffy British guards in full ceremonial dress, complete with buffed black boots and bearskin caps pointing toward the sky that guarded it.

Meanwhile, Ian integrated himself into conversations by eavesdropping. He didn't make introductions, merely listened in on discussions, no doubt cataloguing anything of interest without appearing nosy.

Each passing minute brought the rules, rituals, and required comportment back to her. She must always stand straight, no fidgeting or swaying from side-to-side.

The line moved along at a quick pace, and in less time than it took to cross from one end of her ship to the other, they'd entered the main door. Four footmen were posted inside the doors, taking top hats and coats from guests. She didn't want to leave her mink behind in case they needed to make a quick getaway, but there seemed no other choice.

"*Fraulein?*" A blond, fair-skinned servant stepped forward and extended his arms.

She nodded and turned. It was a chore to stay relaxed as his gloved hands removed the wrap, and she stepped away once her shoulders were free. "*Danke.*"

"*Bitte,*" the footman replied and then moved on to the lady behind her.

When Sorella looked at Ian, he was staring at her bosom. Then he took a few steps away to take in the missing back of her dress.

She tugged his arm, and he came willingly, brushing against her and sparking the latent desire she wanted to ignore. *Damn.*

"Quit pretending like you've never seen this before," she whispered.

"But I haven't," he murmured, smiling at an older couple who walked past them.

"Let's go into the room."

They'd planned to crash the event under the guise of brother and sister, allowing them to stay close to one another with Ian in the role of her chaperone. This ruse would still give them the opportunity to move freely within other circles as needed. If he kept looking at her like a starving man, those false identities would never hold up.

A herald blocked the final set of doors leading into the main room. He called out the names of anyone who entered the room at large. Sorella heard names being announced, though no one of consequence. A viscount here, a lord and lady there, and, finally, it was their turn. Her shoulders were stiff, her body paralyzed at the mere thought of entering the ballroom. It'd been years since she'd performed like this, and nerves were fast to make her believe it'd be impossible to try again after her less-than-appropriate profession.

Her escort separated from her and approached the guardian of the door, whispering their chosen announcement.

When he returned to her side, he squeezed her shoulder. "Relax. You look marvelous." Then he brought her hand to his lips and kissed her knuckles. She swore the kiss somehow touched her bare skin through the layer of silk glove separating them.

Those last words were also pushing their way through her determination to remain cold; making her want to give in to the promises such intimacies with him spoke of.

To make things worse, he trailed his other gloved hand down her exposed shoulder. "Such perfect skin."

She shivered, and then the announcement came.

"May I present Mr. and Mrs. Ian Marshall." The herald's voice filled the air. He moved to the left and let them pass.

"We're supposed to be brother and sister," she said through gritted teeth.

He tucked her arm under his and clasped a hand over hers. "Yes, but since you pointed out my staring, I realized I'd never be able to pull that off. As husband and wife, people will believe the attraction because, let's face it, you've bewitched me."

Into the room, they swept, the long train of her dress trailing behind her. It took a moment for her eyes to adjust because the lighting was much brighter inside this room than anywhere else she'd been recently. The marvel of Tesla was the power behind his vision of electricity. Where America and Edison were plagued with power shortages and even outages, Tesla and his polyphasic alternating current provided stronger, unlimited light, illumination needed to battle against the dark world. If only everyone were allowed to possess it.

Where Janken's club had been an opulent red, the embassy boasted gold-gilded everything. The trim on the walls, chairs on the sides of the room, the draped curtains—the color gold reigned supreme. It made her wonder how much was real and how much paint. No tables in this main room, merely a dancing floor filled with couples twirling to the music. Chairs lined the walls. Open double-doors on the left gave way to another room where refreshments were served. Straight ahead, a half orchestra, strings, horns, and percussion, played on a stage. Loud, lilting music sounded, a classical touch with a sultry, smoky voice providing lyrics to go with it.

The canary, Eva Sonne, stood out in a floor-length, red-beaded dress that shimmered with each shift of her hips. Men stared from the sidelines as couples on the floor moved to the beat in a free-style dance, which was uncommon in the mother country, according to her teachers. Yet here, in this faux British ballroom, they moved out of sync with one another, sashaying from side-to-side or simply swaying back and forth. The movements spoke to her in some primal way, and she wanted to jump out there, to attempt the very same thing.

"If you want to, just say the word."

"How did you know I wanted to dance?"

Ian leaned in, blocking out the cloying smells of cigar smoke, powder, and various perfumes with his own cologne, a citrus scent reminding her of fresh oranges and sitting outdoors on sunny days. "You're tapping your foot in time to the music."

"It's catching." She inhaled sharply as his arm circled her waist.

"Yes, even more so when you're on the floor." He guided her toward the center of the room and twirled her around to face him.

Like the night before, the motions came effortlessly. His hand on her waist, her hand atop his shoulder with their opposites clasping. When he moved, she followed, gliding across the floor, a smooth experience compared to the previous night's practice in her heels. These floors were polished until gleaming, so slippers moved smoothly, and boots didn't scuff.

She let herself get lost in his arms, just as she had during practice, except this time, she focused her attention on his cravat, his fancy tie covering up the thatch of hair she'd seen behind it. For a moment, she'd been afforded the chance to forget her past, the opportunity to be a woman dancing.

They'd traversed the entire floor and were on a second pass when the song changed. Miss Sonne launched into a pretty round of verse and encouraged the guests to begin the waltz. Sorella let Ian lead, moving her effortlessly. "You're very good at this, in case I didn't properly compliment you before."

When Ian didn't respond right away, she snuck a glance at him. Instead of gazing at her, he eyed the stage where Eva Sonne was performing. "All right, I got her attention."

Foolishness had struck again. Her damned, fanciful thoughts never led to anything productive.

"How do you know?" she asked, angling her head to the side to get a glimpse of the canary herself, shaped like an hour glass, a white mink stole draped over her shoulders and short black hair framing her face in the latest style.

"She tugged on her ear."

Sorella scoffed, not bothering to hide her irritation. "A little obvious. Anyone could catch that signal."

"Oh?"

She had his attention now.

He pulled her close, definitely closer than dance rules called for. His warm breath caressed the shell of her ear as he whispered, "What would be your signal?"

"Wouldn't you like to know?" Her lips near his ear lobe, she nipped it. Anything to make him feel as vulnerable as he'd made her.

Chapter Eleven

Ian was trying so hard to be good, but the world-at-large seemed to be working against him. His intentions had been to leave her alone as her first mate and cook had requested, to steer clear of fanning her sexual enticement, to stick to business.

The tempting, gorgeous picture Sorella painted with her backless dress and low cut bodice didn't help matters. Neither did her latest statement and the nip she'd given him. Her intent was pretty clear.

If it weren't for his inherent sense of honor and his parents' rules, he'd be sweeping her into a dark corner or behind a potted plant to kiss her senseless. The proper thing to do would be to ignore his feelings, evade temptation, and focus on the job at hand. The devilish part of him, the same part that had driven his desire to pursue black market merchant work, and had ultimately led to his downfall, refused to be silenced.

"Maybe you can tell me all about it when we get back to the ship." He winked. "Along with all the other secrets you'll be sharing."

"You're extremely confident this woman will know something besides how to mesmerize men in a crowd."

He'd been watching Eva again as she signaled with her eyes the side of the room where she wanted to meet. "She's Luther's main squeeze. She'll know everything. We'll meet up with her after the song."

"How do you know that? Did she shake her rump

at you?"

Too much anger came with those questions, and then he noticed Sorella's pouty expression, lips pursed outward, eyes narrowed. "Are you jealous of a singer?"

She shook her head, ducking her gaze. "The concept is absurd."

"The blush on those cheeks tells a different story."

Before she could respond, the song ended, and he brought them to a halt. They separated, performing the customary bow. Then she replied, "Lead me to her. I want to get this over with."

He moved them across the room, happy to know that his captain still succumbed to basic human emotions. He'd love to tell her how charming her envious streak was. The most he'd shared with Eva had been a kiss months ago, which had led to nothing. Although gorgeous, she failed to inspire any strong desire in him. Lack of time and the surrounding crowd equaled a poor environment to confess such things, but he'd do it once they were back on board the *Liberté*.

As soon as they reached the stage's edge, he heard his name on a whisper, "Ian, come to the left."

He reached back to link his fingers with his captain's, locking their gloved hands together. Strange how, a week prior, he'd never wanted someone tagging along with him on the random jobs he did for *The Cursed*, but this one connection gave him a sense of reassurance and strength he normally didn't possess on such outings. Now he couldn't imagine entering a situation without this dangerous woman at his side. *Hell, I'm becoming attached.*

They walked between two flowering trees positioned at the stage side and found a small table with three chairs. The singer stood next to one, arms open. "*Kauffman*." Merchant. "It's been a long time."

"Indeed," he tugged on his captain's connection with him to bring her around from behind. "Miss Sonne, may I introduce the captain of the *Liberté*."

"You have his eyes." Eva stared at her hard, looking Sorella up and down. Shock clearly lined her face.

"Whose?"

"Your father's. I've met him a few times right here in this very club." The woman adopted another polite smile.

A tightness rose in her chest. This woman's familiarity with her visage damned them. Everything would be wrecked. "Is he here tonight?"

"No, but he was here the other night."

Ian looked between them, confused. "Who's her father?"

"That's not what we came here to talk about," she said, patting his hand. Her secrets were hers to reveal to whomever—whenever—she wanted. Too bad Bonita's hairdressing job hadn't been good enough and that Sorella's looks were so singular. At some point, they'd need to at least address the possibility of other people recognizing her.

"Right." Ian took over. "I have a bounty for Luther and need to find him."

"One moment." The vocalist gestured to the guard behind her. She whispered something to him, and Sorella caught the name of her ship included in the exchange.

The captain waited for Eva's security to depart then queried, "Why are you discussing my ship?"

Eva's eyes went wide, and she fluttered a hand to her collarbone. The woman did a fantastic job of appearing fragile and dainty, but those gray eyes showed a steely nature, no doubt as immovable as a mountain when the time called for it. "I've sent my man to alert your ship to come here for you."

"Planning ahead. I like how you think." This woman feared the same thing she did, that her disguise had been useless and no doubt the *polizei* were being alerted as they spoke. "Will you tell us where he is?"

The singer shook her head. "Not until *he*," she nodded at Ian, "answers my questions." She turned to look at him. "Why do you need me to tell you this? Luther would've given you a rendezvous."

Ian let go of Sorella and moved toward the singer, donning an arrogant smile, his eyes hooded. This was the man who flattered and spun tales, the one she wanted nothing to do with. Did he play the same cards with her, and she'd just been too blind to see?

"Eva, dear." He took her hand and bowed over it. "He gave me a rendezvous, but tracking this bounty took longer than planned."

"And Patrick in Nordberg? He would've gladly told you where to go."

Shit. The man she'd knifed without a care. Now the canary would never sing for them. "He was captured and taken by inspectors. No doubt he's been interrogated and silenced. They picked him up right as I got to town. Trust me, I don't want to ask you, but I've got no choice. This is the last favor, and the last time I'll ever put you in danger."

When had a man other than Bastille ever lied for her? A lump lodged in her throat, dropping to her stomach as the singer let out a shrill laugh.

"Danger? From you? This girl is more dangerous than you ever were. Stupid idea to bring her here. It will take pure luck for you to get out of the embassy alive."

Then she turned those kohl lined, gray eyes on Sorella and narrowed them. She bunched the ends of her white fur stole between clenched fists, her high cheek bones flushed. Even angry, this woman looked majestic.

"You know the threat she poses. Everyone wants to get a hold of her...if they can. Why not trade? I'll tell you where Luther is if you give me her. My place in the embassy isn't secure. They are always worried about spies. I'd be able to prove my worth." Her smile was purely feral, not fragile at all, but as bent at the core as so many in the world. She was also extremely self-reliant. No wonder Luther admired her.

"I can't, Eva. Without her, the ship won't fly. I'd be dead attempting to board without the captain by my side."

The woman shrugged her shoulders. "Eh, figured as much, but had to give it a try."

"What do you want for the information?" Sorella asked. No use beating the topic to death. If they were in for a fight, she'd rather start her way toward the exit now.

Instead of a quick answer, Eva adjusted her dress

114

and trimmed the edges of her mouth with an index finger and thumb. She was drawing their encounter out, making things worse. *Enough.* Sorella moved, striking like a snake suddenly uncoiled. She latched onto Eva's wrist and twisted, holding her hand at an awkward angle. With one tweak, the delicate bone would snap in two.

"Ow! Let go." The exclamation was half-hearted, more for show than anything.

"I don't have any more time for amusements. You may enjoy high-risk, dangerous situations, but I've got plans for my future. Now tell us where he is."

"I wouldn't joke with her," Ian chimed in. "I've seen her stab people for less."

The canary smiled, respect in her eyes. "So have I. Definitely appreciate a lady who's not quite a lady. Let me go, and I'll tell you."

Instinct told her to cut her losses, but she remembered what Ian had said about less being more, and how she should let a threat do the work for her. "If you're playing, I'll break your arm."

"I'd expect no less." The words were without artifice, and in the same smoky voice she used on stage.

Sorella released the singer and stepped back, closer to the one person in the room she could trust. He didn't hesitate to wrap an arm around her and squeeze her shoulder. *Have I impressed him?*

"Luther is hiding on the Isle of Grimsey, north of Iceland."

"Why the hell is he hiding there?" Ian lifted a brow.

"Would you look for him in a place where the

average temperature is barely above freezing?" The singer parried. Sorella would've looked anywhere, even unlikely places, if the source was solid. Anywhere equaled a place to hide and how well you evaded detection came down to your disguise.

"Thank you, Miss Sonne." *Time to go.* "Now, how do we get out of here?"

***

He wanted to crow when they learned *The Cursed*'s location. He'd never admit that, for a moment, he'd thought she wouldn't tell them. In that brief second, he'd believed the singer wanted them to be caught.

Instead, holding a small lamp in front of her, she guided them through a narrow back passageway with twists and turns everywhere, most likely one of many secret corridors inside the embassy. The possibility still existed that she'd turn on them; give them up for whatever reassurances she could gain. He understood the need for security. Luther's dish had been discarded before. Hell, every time the man left her, she swore up and down she'd never be abandoned again.

"Your ship will be on the roof," Eva said, grabbing a fistful of red beaded gown in each hand before she started up the staircase which loomed before them.

Sorella followed, and Ian took up the rear, glancing back every few steps, searching for pursuers. He'd embrace the *Liberté*'s deck if they made it out alive, and he'd make sure he kissed his captain.

After their conversation with Eva, he had even

116

more questions than he'd had earlier in the day. He was still dealing with the irony that everyone recognized her but him. He, the pride of New Orleans, heir to one of the founding bloodlines of the city, had failed to identify someone everyone knew.

They'd made it up the second flight of stairs when his captain stopped and looked over the railing. "They're coming," she whispered. "Hurry."

No sense in being quiet as they clipped their way upward. Raised voices floated up from beneath them, voices calling out in Deutsch for them to halt, to surrender to the kaiser. He'd rather jump to his death than be strung up in some work camp.

Then he saw the spark. German enemies held electo wands in their hands. One touch to the metal staircase, and they'd be done for. Time to deploy Bastille's EMP grenade. He stopped on the next landing, lifted his shoe, and slid open the compartment on the heel.

"What are you doing?" Sorella asked, running back down toward him.

He waved her away with his free hand. "Keep going. I'll be right behind you."

For once, she didn't remind him who was in charge or question his decisions. She dashed past him, slinging her dress train over her shoulder. He smiled at the pretty view he won of her ankles. If everything went as planned....

He grabbed the top and bottom of the small grenade with both hands, pulled, and turned each section opposite the other. One click meant the bomb was armed. Then he leaned over the edge and dropped it down.

Clambering up the stairs, he heard the bomb go off. The angry shouts confirmed that the deterrent worked. As he looked up, the girls were pushing open the door to the roof. Only a few more flights, and he'd be right there with them.

Then a revolver cocked, the sound of the chamber rotating into place halting him. "Stop, *dieb*!" Stop, thief.

"Germans shouldn't play with American weapons." Ian turned and raised his hands in the air to signal surrender. Sure enough, a soldier was training a gun right on him. These guys packed more than the typical electric based weapons preferred by the kaiser.

A high pitched whistle rent the air, and the sharp end of a silver balisong pierced the soldier through the heart. No helping it. The dead man's reflexes triggered the gun, and Ian dropped to the floor, hoping the bullet missed him.

His remaining charge up those steps went without incident, and he enjoyed the fresh, chilly night air that hit his face as he emerged onto the roof. Eva stood by the door, and Sorella already had an arm wrapped around a platform disc tether.

"I'm sorry, Eva. Maybe you should come with us. You're not safe."

A single shake of her head. "No. Luther wanted me to stay, to gather intel. I'll weasel my way out of this. But I want you to give him a message for me."

Eva deserved better than that, so much better.

"Anything."

"Tell him I'm only waiting two more weeks. If he doesn't come, I'm gone, and I'll sell whatever I know to the highest bidder."

118

He nodded in agreement, and that's when another shot rang out, this time from above.

The singer's body dropped, and he saw blood beginning to seep out of a wound on her right arm, staining her mink. "Eva!"

"No," she waved him away. "I told her to make it believable. Get out of here."

Ian dashed for the other platform, wrapped his gloved hand around the twined steel, and looked on with regret. Abandoning a woman wasn't part of his code. The guilt twisted his insides like the coiling ropes on board the ship above him.

The soldiers stormed onto the roof right after he'd been pulled aboard. The ship took off with a burst of speed, reaching a high altitude in no time, soaring above the clouds that had rolled in since they'd been inside.

He never saw whether they'd grabbed the singer, but she'd weathered many storms. He'd deliver her message to Luther and pray the man wised up.

Chapter Twelve

Sorella crossed herself, thankful the merchant had made it on board safely. She tossed the rifle to Bastille and proceeded toward her helmsman, Gustave. He'd been with her since the beginning, another cast-off from the war. Missing one leg, he stood on a metal replacement and, never one to complain, looked at her now, a question in his eyes. He'd fought against the kaiser's armies, faced those weapons. She understood if he never wanted to see a battle again.

"Our heading, Captain?" he asked. His gruff voice matched his low-brow wool cap and gray beard.

"The Isle of Grimsey, north of Iceland."

He nodded and pointed the bow north toward the sea and away from danger. "Will this be the last stop?"

Rarely did he talk beyond asking which direction the ship needed to head, so when he spoke, she usually listened. If he queried, she replied, but for this question, there was no answer. "I don't know."

Her thoughts wandered to Ian, to the horrific look on his face when Eva fell. For a moment, she'd believed there'd been something between them, some emotional attachment. Why else would he risk precious time and potentially his own life to check on a woman who'd threatened their safety?

Even now, the merchant appeared out of sorts, tugging at his cravat and undoing the elegant knot to reveal the thatch of hair she'd imagined during their dance. She needed to get the hell out of this dress and quit worrying about a man's inclinations, which seemed to be as unpredictable as the weather.

She patted Gustave on the shoulder. "Stay warm, and have me alerted once we've passed Britain."

"Aye, aye."

Then she headed for her cabin. Her shoes had cut into her heels for the last part of their adventure although the adrenaline of their escape had made her numb to the worst of it. Her body had calmed down since then, and now the pads of her feet ached along with her heels. Time to rest, quietly rejoice the day's conquests, and repent her sins. *The Cursed* were within their grasp. A day's trip, since the ship's speed was slower in the colder climate. Her technicians had assured her that to run hot risked dangers she didn't want to deal with.

Once in the corridor, she hiked up her train, keeping it clear of her feet, and shuffled toward her room. Heavy boots sounded from behind her, clipping toward her with a determined pace.

"Captain?" Ian called out.

She stopped in front of her door and turned. "What do you want?"

A bit of an attitude, yes, but she had good reason. The bastard had lied to her.

"All the things you promised me," he said, quirking the left side of his mouth into some devious half-smile that did strange things to her pulse.

What about Eva? "Really? Why cast aside your worries about the one we left behind?"

He trailed a finger down her cheek then. "What are you talking about?"

"Your connection to the canary. You nearly risked your life for her back there."

"My poor assassin," he clucked as fingers became a hand caressing her bare shoulder. "You've truly never known caring. I'd do the same for anyone risking their life for me. No special connection is needed beyond them putting themselves on the line, the same as me."

"And you're not angry?"

He leaned in and nipped at her ear lobe, sending a ripple of want through her body. "Whatever gave you that idea?"

"I shot Eva."

"It's only an arm shot, and I know the reason for it." The words caressed her, lulled her into a desirous haze. "And you liked it."

Goose bumps broke out on her skin at the thought. Yes, she'd enjoyed it as much as she relished the way his body pressed up against hers. Then want compounded into some hot, messy thing as he kissed the same flesh he'd gripped in his hand.

She fumbled for the knob behind her. A few blind attempts, and, finally, she turned it, pushed the door open, and backed away from him. Her chest tightened at the predatory stare he leveled at her, so unlike his playful self.

Yet he didn't move forward. "Can I come in?"

Her only response, a single nod. The best she could do, her mouth having gone dry minutes before when he'd put his lips on her body. A bad idea for sure, but no sense in denying she wanted him like this, was ravenous for his attention and heated gaze. She'd been ignored as a child and eagerly cast aside for political goals. She'd been taught to discard her wants for the greater good, to seek only pleasure in pain.... Those ideals were rapidly burning away like smoke in the wind.

The door shut behind him, cutting off the world and sealing them in darkness except for the moon shining through her porthole. She prepared for him to charge her, to leap on her in desperation. Instead, he flicked the switch and bathed the room in light.

"That dress has been a source of extreme discomfort for me tonight."

She slipped her shoes off, stepping down to the bare, cold floor. "Why?"

"It's showing me everything I've been missing. You're normally wrapped up in clothes that cover every patch of skin." He prowled forward, removing his dress jacket and tossing it behind him. "This," his hands caressed her body through her beaded gown, tracing the outline of her figure and making her knees go weak, "provides more for my imagination."

As quickly as he'd started, he backed away. "Tell me who your father is?"

Drawing several quick breaths, she attempted to slow her pulse as she took a seat in front of her vanity. She'd kill his amorous ambitions with this confession for sure. "My father is the Prime Minister of Italy, Marcello Corvino."

"The same prime minister whose daughter is supposed to marry the son of the President of the United States in less than six months?"

Here came the moment of truth, the moment when he'd learned the worst of it. "I am that daughter."

"You're *the* Sorella Corvino?" He phrased the

words as a question instead of a fact. A hard pill to swallow, judging from the shock on his face.

She nodded and reached up to remove the pins from her hair, the long locks falling in waves to her waist.

A low-lidded gaze replaced his wide eyes, and he approached her with confidence. Spearing his fingers into her hair, he lifted the weight and then allowed gravity to drag the hair down. "Soft, like your skin…and I'm seducing Roosevelt Jr.'s bride-to-be. You're boosting my ego, Captain."

Seduce, a word she'd never used in conjunction with her or her body, a word implying the removal of clothes, the loss of her maidenhead, and the ability to kill this man without guilt. "How do you know I'll let you?"

He knelt beside her. "I don't, but I aim to try. A merchant believes in negotiation and perseverance, especially when seeking to purchase something he desires beyond all other things."

"Am I a thing to be bought?" She arched her back, a mix of want and fear doing strange things to her insides. *Hail Mary*. He was a contradiction of everything she expected. He enjoyed her famous place in the upper echelons and found it humorous. In the same stroke, he compared her to goods to be bought and sold—poor words.

"No, you're a woman to be worshipped." Then all the right ones. "But I have to wonder why you're hiding here, trading for time with cutthroats and the damaged instead of joining your future husband?"

A good question. "Because I refused to sacrifice my body for a political arrangement."

"A very good reason." Then he touched her again, this time grabbing the edge of one glove and pulling it down her arm, exposing her flesh, the move intimate, maddening. Moisture pooled in her vagina, a clinical word she'd learned in her study of human anatomy. To be a killer, one had to identify all parts of the body and understand the pain that could be imparted to each piece.

Yet his little caresses and small actions implied a large amount of pleasure could be dealt as well, unleashing a similar amount of discomfort on one's fragile heart.

The glove peeled off the tips of her fingers, and he discarded it before moving on to the next.

"Do you plan to remove all my clothes without asking me?" Horrible how soft and weak her voice sounded. The commanding tone she normally employed failed her in the face of intimacy, and her knives were across the room. She'd lost one to the stupid soldier on the steps, the bastard who had dared to take away this man, this merchant—nay, this seducer—who moved at the pace of a snail and surveyed every inch of revealed skin with the concentration of a technician.

"Do you want me to?" Crouching beside her, he stopped then, and their eyes met. A flash sparked in his, a challenge he wanted her to meet.

Did she have the courage to go through with this? The ability to abandon herself to an act that would change everything? No more holding on to the possibility her parents would change their minds or the thought that she could escape marriage because people actually cared.

This path did allow her to experience something she'd never had. Something unknown.

"You're overthinking this." He busted through her wandering thoughts. "To say yes only means your clothes come off. Nothing else. Remember…you choose what you want. I stop whenever you tell me to. This one decision doesn't supersede future ones."

Relief flooded through her, coupled with a heavy dose of surprise. He was ceding control to her, the ability to determine each action or at least put a halt to ones she didn't like.

"Then yes."

Ian let out the breath he'd been holding on a slow exhale. He was thankful he had discarded his jacket because the room ran hot. The few clothes on his body were too many, but first he needed to please her.

She'd said yes. To his removing her dress…. To wanting him. Obviously, her hesitance was because of poor care from past lovers. He'd change her mind. Demonstrate how a good paramour gave pleasure instead of taking it.

Moving from his crouch to a standing position, he held a hand out, giving her a second chance to back out or confirm acceptance of his proposal.

Damn. Was his hand shaking?

She embraced his palm with her own, her fingers folding over the pulse point at his wrist, able to feel his pounding pulse for sure. She probably thought he was nervous. Hell, nervous didn't skim the surface. Before him stood a woman hailed as a princess by the kaiser and all his allies. One half of the supposed "marriage that would heal the world."

Standing in front of her, he didn't know for a split second, what to do or say. Her hair flowed about her, black as a raven's wings. A pink blush spread through her cheeks and down her neck. A warrior of the sky, a monarch of death, and he wanted her with every piece of his battered soul. Now to make sure she didn't change her mind.

He let go of her, swept the curtain of her hair to one side, and hooked his thumbs under the straps of her dress. "Are you ready?"

As soon as the words were out, he regretted them, but her eyes blazed with desire instead of mirth. She smiled and nodded. Her skin was hot beneath his touch as he dragged the straps off her shoulders. The bodice fell, baring her pale breasts with two small, dark, cherry-colored nipples.

Tasting them became a priority, and he bent to pull one into his mouth. Then he grasped the tip between his teeth, exerting a little pressure, but not a full-on bite.

She gasped. "*Buon Dio!*" Good God.

"Do you like it?" he quizzed, words a bit muffled since he was still latched to her, lapping her skin to sooth his rough treatment.

"More," she moaned.

Never say Ian Marshall didn't follow his captain's instructions. He blessed both breasts with a thorough tonguing, reveling in her response, so sensitive and damned erotic. When he finally moved away, he saw a smile he could only contribute to extreme arousal.

"What now?" She wanted more.

"Now we remove the dress completely—"

She effectively cut him off, shimmying the beaded

gown past her hips and stepping out without preamble. A small rounded belly, flared hips, and a thatch of dark hair between her legs rendered him speechless. Was there ever a more beautiful body to match such a miraculous soul? No, he didn't believe so.

Then he knew what he wanted to do. Worship her, as he'd mentioned before. "Climb onto the bed."

"Why?" She put one hand on her waist and eyed him with speculation.

"The better to worship you, Captain." Those words garnered him a smile and compliance. She sauntered to the bed with slow, sensual steps that, if possible, made his cock harden even more. He followed, and once she sat, dropped to his knees. Placing a hand on either thigh, he pushed outward, delighted when she spread her legs…for him.

"My mouth is going to pleasure you now, Captain. Tell me if it's too much." Then he moved in, thumbs and forefingers spreading her lips to reveal her clit, a nub he flicked with his tongue.

She groaned with approval, and he continued his onslaught, long slow strokes from her opening to the top, followed with short, rapid lashings, until finally he needed a full taste of her and inserted his tongue. He shivered at the idea of part of him being where, hopefully, his cock would be soon.

As he mimicked the motions of lovemaking with his tongue, he could hear her panting. Her release was imminent, her body restless underneath him. Legs wrapped around his waist, she bucked against him as if attempting to get closer. When she finally cried out his name, a rush of arousal coated his tongue She tasted so good, he refused to let any of it go to waste and lapped it up like the gift it was.

Pulling back, he grinned. She looked fully debauched, hair spread against the bed covers, chest heaving. "I never…."

"What?"

"Knew you could do that." She propped herself up on her elbows, a playful expression on her face.

"You've had some very inconsiderate lovers."

Sitting up, her smile became a frown.

"What's wrong?" He couldn't lose her now.

"I haven't had any."

"Excuse me?" She led a ship full of disreputable men, lived a dangerous life, and to discover no one had ever worshipped her body, shown it praise as it deserved—a tragedy. "How is this possible?"

She tugged her knees up under her chin, and Ian rose to sit on the end of the bed. "I'm a virgin bride meant to marry the son of the country who prizes innocence over everything else. Why would I have lovers?"

Too true. Yet she was a killer, an inflictor of pain and death. He'd falsely assumed such a provocation required a sexual release. Tense situations usually left him seeking the oblivion an orgasm granted if only for a few moments.

"I understand." Ian stroked his chin. "Do you want to keep it…erm, your virginity, that is?"

"I have my reasons for remaining this way."

"Care to share?"

Stretching her legs out again, he tried to ignore her body, the moisture still clinging to her nether hair. She rubbed her feet against the soft blanket underneath them and spoke softly, "I'd be able to marry with or without my hymen intact, but giving that part of me to someone requires a connection far deeper than a simple friendship. I'd have to want that."

He understood what she meant, though in his experience, sexual romps didn't require emotional commitment. Yet his first always held a special place in his heart. Why not the same with a woman? If the concern lay with the connection between two people and not the societal norms imposed by their respective homelands, there remained a chance he'd help her open up.

"Some believe that having sex creates a bond, but that doesn't mean you're tied to someone for the rest of your life. Like anyone you love, the experience will create fond memories."

"Were you loved as a child?" She bent her head to one side, arms and hands propping her up on the bed.

"My family was close, if that's what you mean." Closer than most in society's opinion, for his mother and father loved each other.

"Mine sent me to tutors from a young age. I spent most of my time either learning to inflict pain or having it exacted on me. Christmas presents and birthday gifts were either beautiful clothes or weapons."

How cruel to only be taught how to deliver death and agony or receive it. "No one told you they loved you or showed you pleasure?"

"Those moments were few and far between. The only person who made it bearable was my brother. He gave me hope and a belief in concepts like fun and laughter. Then he was stolen from me, and I lost that closeness."

Ian stood, moving to free the buttons on his shirt. He shrugged out of the garment at a rapid pace and proceeded to his trousers. No more sad discussions or reliving horrible memories. He'd give her new ones filled with joy.

"What are you doing?" Sorella sat up completely now at full alert.

He grinned. "Removing my clothes. It's not fair if you're naked, and I'm not."

She stared openly, no false smiles or sly grins, just honest curiosity, and his cock loved it, straining against his cotton underwear, aroused to a painful degree.

"I haven't seen a—a male part before."

"You don't have to be afraid of the word cock, Captain," he said shoving his drawers to the floor. He stood gloriously naked and empowered, thanks to her continued perusal of his form. She was especially focused on said cock.

"How do we do this?" She sounded confident, but the tremble he'd seen pass through her body moments ago told him otherwise.

"I'll tell you what," he climbed back onto the bed and began prowling slowly toward her on all fours. "You lean back against the pillows behind you, and I'll worry about mechanics. I want you to indulge and have fun."

Laying back as he'd asked her to, she stiffened her body in anticipation. He spread out beside her, tweaking one nipple between two fingers. She moaned, her posture becoming more languid. "I like that."

He bent over her, taking the same tipped point into his mouth and suckling from it. "I believe I can show you more things you'll like."

"Will it hurt?"

He looked up, softened by the genuine concern in her voice. "Are you afraid of pain?"

"Never."

"Then you have nothing to worry about."

Sorella thought she'd lose her mind. The sensations and tingling in her vagina were foreign, but not unappreciated, as Ian nursed from her breasts, tugging and laving each nipple until they were so sensitive she could…no, did let out a small scream.

"Would you like me to move on to something else?" he asked with a chuckle, and then put his fingers through her nether hair, touching the small nub at the top of her vagina.

"I ache," she replied.

"Here?" He rubbed her again.

She nodded. "More."

The pressure built quickly, pulse pounding in her ears. Surely, she'd die. Within minutes, she called out his name as everything exploded. Her vision blurred, and she knew nothing but pleasure. "What did you do to me?"

He moved now, spreading her legs and seating himself in between them. "I've heard it called many things. Most commonly an orgasm, though the French call it *La Petite Mort*." *The small death.*

"Yes, I can see why."

He inserted a finger into her opening. "You're so

wet. Dare I believe you're ready for more?"

Was she? Already her heart felt too big for her chest, blood pulsing at every main artery, and, hell, if she didn't experience the stirrings of a new arousal as he added a second finger to the first. "Yes, please."

The words came out low and needy. Then the fingers were gone, replaced with the head of his cock. He rubbed it up and down over her opening, coating himself in the remnant of her last orgasm. If she had another one in her, it would be miracle.

Forward movement came slowly. With each half-inch of penetration, he stopped, allowing her body to stretch and accommodate his girth. Not horribly wide, per se, but enough so that when he finally broke the wall of her hymen, he wasn't fully seated just yet.

She didn't scream, just waited, and he looked at her for acknowledgement. Always caring about her. Were all men so considerate, the world would be a much different place.

"Move, please," she begged.

So he did, plunging forward with a groan. Full, so full and marvelous. Then he pulled away, and she struggled to keep him there.

"Sweet Captain."

"No, my name. Say it," she said through gritted teeth as he moved in and out, setting a fast paced drive as if in a race; against what, she didn't know. Then he leaned down and pulled her up so she sat on his lap. Grabbing her hips, he lifted her up and down on him. She took the moment to grab his face with both hands and join their mouths.

The kiss turned from simple lips meeting to ravenous tongues, nips of teeth, and moans of passion. He pounded into her from below and devoured her from above. She'd never felt so insane, so absolutely out of control, or so desired in all her life. Orgasm threatened, building quickly as they continued to move.

"It's coming."

"Sorella," her name was a whispered invocation against her lips.

She saw stars; the world went black. Then he threw her off him, back against the pile of pillows, taking himself in hand as his own release spurted forth onto her thighs.

As the last shudder racked his frame, he let go of himself and rose from the bed, moving away from her. Laying there, she began to doubt what they'd shared, doubt his words. Then he came back with a warm, damp cloth.

"What's that for?"

"To clean up the mess I made." He wiped her thighs clean, then moved away to discard the rag. "I didn't hurt you, did I?"

All the uncertainty disappeared. Sorella was awed again by his concern, his blatant caring for her and not himself. She shook her head, and he climbed back to her, wrapping his arms around her and pulling her close.

The position was strange and new, but, like the intimacy they'd just shared, she wanted the closeness.

"Has anyone held you for comfort?"

"No. Whenever I was afraid of something, I was forced to face it." A small lie; she didn't want to recall those moments where her brother had hugged her and sang her stories, not when she'd just had the most wonderful experience.

Instead, she chased away the memories by snuggling against Ian, loving the way his breath warmed her neck and how he provided a wall of strength because he wanted to, not because it was needed.

He reached down and pulled the covers that had been pushed to the end of the bed over them. "What were you afraid of?"

"I had a fear of heights. So I was taught to walk bridges and ropes over high spaces."

"That's horrible. Your parents were evil."

"Fear is simply a brain function designed to inhibit your abilities. In some ways, their approach made me stronger. Faster. More capable." She could stand in a pit of vipers, survive in small, enclosed spaces, and disassemble a brick wall because she had mastered her fears.

Ian pressed a kiss to her neck, then her collarbone, each touch feather-light and already kindling fresh arousal. "While I find your strength admirable, you don't have to fell every obstacle."

"That's what they wanted me to do. To be able to kill with ease and maneuver out of any trap or trouble. I'm bred for that purpose."

"Do you want such a purpose?" His voice was low and soft as he stroked her hair, lulling her into a cocoon of peace. For the first time in…ever…she felt safe.

"No." Her eyes closed. All the lovemaking had worn her out. "I want to take care of my crew. To roam the skies and simply be free."

"Me, too, Sorella."

Then she let herself drift to sleep.

Chapter Thirteen

A pounding on the door brought her to a sitting position. She rubbed her eyes and looked down to see Ian's arms still wrapped around her waist. Daylight streamed in through the porthole, bright and unfettered by clouds. The hammering continued in earnest.

"Captain!" Bastille's voice resonated through the door. "We're being pursued!"

Sorella jumped out of bed and sprinted to her dressing screen across the room, shoving her body into undergarments and all her usual wear. "Come in!"

The doors opened per her command, slamming against the walls, the sound echoing.

Ian's voice rang out, loud and drowsy, "What's going on?"

"There's a ship gaining on us fast, Captain. We can't identify it, but they Morsed one message." Her first mate paused.

She pulled her shirt over her head and fastened the vest into place. "Don't keep me in suspense."

"Surrender Tuul."

She emerged from behind the screen with her lover still in bed, sitting upright and looking worried. "Don't worry. We won't go down without a fight." The *Liberté* had plenty of tricks, thanks to ingenious engineering and the upgrades some extremely talented technicians had added to the mix. "How big is the challenger?"

"Same size as ours."

Meaning the crew complement rested at roughly forty or less. Even forty was a big number for a vessel their size. She kept the numbers at thirty-five, leaving cabins open for last minute passengers and the like. "Then let's—"

The annoying ring of the attack siren cut her off, bellowing down the ship's corridors.

"Bastille," she yelled, "I'll meet you on deck."

He nodded and ran from the room. Once the man was out of sight, Ian jumped off the bed and grabbed his clothes. "So much for breakfasting in the room."

Of course, he would find a way to be relaxed in the face of such a challenge. She grabbed her balisong from the nightstand and shoved it in one holster, then crossed to the valise to retrieve her spare. "I love how you can joke. Those alarms mean—"

"EMP. Yes, I've been on a ship under attack before. Where do you want me?" He'd snuck behind her, hands gripping her arms in a tender embrace. She froze. Suddenly pleasure and business were blurring and juggling. Both became an impossible feat for the moment. Ian sensed her confusion and let go.

She rounded on him and gave him a peck to the cheek to apologize. "I'm sorry. I can't think when you do that."

"No worries. Where do you want me?"

The hurt in his eyes would have to wait until later. "They want Tuul, so head to the brig. We need to keep him secure."

"Aye, aye, Captain." The honorific was bestowed with a wink, then he left, hoisting his coat from the chair on his way out. She stood for a moment…. In

138

her case, one too many. The first EMP blast hit, and time seemed to momentarily freeze; a low sound, like the striking of a gong, echoed through the ship, ceasing as the pulse dissipated. Thank the stars for the new shields with wood and rubber rivet grafting.

She sprinted out of the room, headed for the deck. Nearing the door, she heard shouts, and then the whole ship went dark. The vessel lurched left. Following the course of gravity, she slammed into the wall, cursing as the hallway bulbs blinked out completely. They were still airborne, but the EMP had affected all the other systems. She pushed off the wall and pulled open the barrier separating her from her crew. Emerging from the corridor, she had to duck back in immediately to miss an electo-pulse from a hand-held coil. Shots were flying all over the place. Sheer luck they hadn't set the boat on fire.

Bastille was straight in front of her, grappling with the electo-net, a new protective option they'd yet to employ. She dashed out, pushing aside her fear of being struck by a few volts of electricity, to help Bastille get the upper hand.

Reaching her first mate, she pushed his hands away from the mechanism. "You've got the line tangled around the gear." She whipped out a balisong to cut the string attached near the bronze gear shaft. Then the net flew loose. A high-pitched whining sound rent the air as the next piece spread and encompassed the top deck. The miracle in the mesh was the rubber blended wire expanding up and out from the pole, acting as a lightning rod to catch electric pulses and dispel them before they hurt anyone or started a fire. The crew cheered.

"Fire the EMP," Sorella hollered, but to no avail since Gustav was engaged in his own battle. She and Bastille scrambled to the helmsman's deck. Popping open the casing at the bottom of the steering wheel, she flipped the switch for the starboard side cannon. The lighting grid under the switch burned red. It would take at least a minute for the light to turn green, giving the go-ahead.

Another explosion. Wood flew through the air, and metal screeched as a grappling hook tore through the hull. Their guest's generosity knew no bounds, and soon three hands were using the rope to slide from the attacking ship to the *Liberté*. They sliced through the net and hopped aboard.

She slapped her first mate on the shoulder. "You stay here until the EMP is ready and then fire. I don't give two shits and a giggle if they all die." For tearing a hole in her ship, they deserved it. "I'm going to make sure those three don't make it to Tuul."

"Aye, aye."

Then she launched off again, taking the steps back to the lower deck two at time, and swinging herself over the railing to bypass the last few. Landing on her feet, she moved in the direction her unwanted guests had gone, past the door to the ship's main corridor and down the port side. When she reached the rear of the ship, they'd disappeared. Only then did she notice the smaller grappling hooks clinging to the railing. They'd gone straight to the brig dropping to it from the back of the ship.

A peek over the edge, and, sure enough…. A nice gaping hole, sliced out with an electo wand, gave a perfect view of one man, a lookout. Sorella leaned up, took a deep breath, and then, without hesitation, gripped a grappling rope with one gloved hand and swung herself over, aiming for the corner of the opening. Her aim was true, and she brought booted heels to her enemy's chest, felling him immediately.

Her lover lay on the floor, unconscious. Fear clawed at her heart, and she charged toward him. "Ian! Wake up!"

Just as she neared him, a big, meaty arm encircled her waist and threw her back into the wall. The pain was negligible, and she drew her balisongs. "Let me make your smiles permanent, *bastardos*."

No one was getting out of here alive.

His mouth was dry, and a throbbing headache radiated through his skull. He heard Sorella yelling at him to wake up. Hell, if only they were back in her bed away from the men and the fighting…. *Shit! Tuul.*

Ian's eyes flew open, and he pushed himself up off the floor. No time to cry over a little pain. Then one of Sorella's knives slid over and hit his boot, handle-first. She let out a struggled grunt, both arms wrestling for control against her attacker, a man three times her size.

He reached down for the knife. When he looked up, the bounty hunter had pulled a gun and aimed. Sorella lost her footing and fell. For a moment, time suspended and the idea of her being shot had him seeing red like one of the bulls in the fighting rings of Spain.

Charging forward, he stuck the idiot in his back, not once or twice, but four times in the region of the kidneys on either side. The gun clattered onto the floor, and the bounty hunter fell forward, failing to fire a single shot. Sorella scrambled away to avoid being pinned under the body.

He'd killed a man, taken the life of someone who may have been good or bad.

"Thank you," she said, patting his arm. "Are you okay?"

"Yes." He nodded and mumbled, unable to stop staring at the body or the darkened stain on the shirt where blood was pooling.

"Where's Tuul?"

The question pulled him away from the corpse on the floor, and he glanced around the room. The cell door was swinging open, the cage empty. "When the EMP knocked out the power briefly, he ambushed me and made a run for it."

"There was one more hunter.... Did you see him?"

"No." Ian had been out for more than a few minutes then. She swore and ran out of the room. He followed, hoping his bounty hadn't been captured or killed. He needed the bastard alive, even if the fool wanted to hurt everyone.

A scream came from the direction of the kitchen, and he stayed on his captain's heels until they reached the entrance. Another carcass blocked their way. Not one of the crew though. Based on the clothes, another bounty hunter. A puddle of red near the man's head told him all he needed to know.

In the mess of the usually neat kitchen, Ian searched frantically for Bonita and Gretchen. Then he saw the cook trapped underneath a chair, eyes wide with fear. Gretchen wasn't with her.

A scuffling sound made Ian look up. Tuul stood at the far edge of the room, his hands around Gretchen's throat. "You think you'll keep me locked up, tossers? Well, that's the last mistake you make with me. Step back, both o' you, or I snap the filly's neck."

"You don't want to do that. We'll let you stay in a cabin until the trip is over." He didn't need to look at Sorella to know she disagreed with his suggestion. "Hell, even got a snipe for you. Just put the girl down, and we'll stay right here."

Tension weighted the air like the humidity in New Orleans on an early spring day. No one moved for a long moment, and then everyone moved at once.

"I think I'll take my chances." The scag uttered the last word as Sorella's blade launched from her hand.

Ian cried out and made for the captain's hand, but too late. Gretchen screamed, dropping to the floor. No one cared about the dead man who'd been his only shot at freedom, his only chance to finally pay the debt he owed to *The Cursed* for breaking him out of jail and smuggling him away from his bloodthirsty cousin.

Bastille pushed him aside. Both captain and first mate assisted the ladies while he slunk to the floor, his thoughts filled with anger, disappointment, and sadness. Helping Sorella and the crew of the *Liberté* meant accepting the madness of the morning, the insanity of Tuul's mind, and the quick-fire decisions of his captain.

Sitting there, he realized no matter how doomed his future may be, the die had been cast, and there was no going back.

Chapter Fourteen

Now that Sorella had finally held true to her word and let her vengeance fly on Tuul, all signs of conflict were removed and order restored. Thankfully, her crew came away with few injuries, and once Bastille communicated to the attacking vessel that their hunters were dead along with their bounty, they'd flown off.

Time to change clothes, to wash the grime, sweat, and blood from her body. She strode into her cabin, heading straight for her vanity. Steam wafted from the pitcher through the air as she poured a measure of water into the basin bowl. Without preamble, she shoved her hands into the water, loving how the clear substance washed away the impure ones from her skin. Once her hands were clean, she shed her vest, then her boots, and stood in her darned socks on the cool floor.

"I can't believe you killed him." Ian's voice was low and came from the direction of her bed.

"Why are you in here?" She reached for a clean cloth and dipped it into the pitcher.

"This is the only place I know we can talk in private."

"He was an awful man, if you could call him a man."

The bed creaked as he rose and crossed the room, the spurs on his boots like death knocks spelling the end of them as lovers. "He was my ticket to freedom."

"What are you talking about?" She put the scrap to her neck and wiped away the grime on the front and back.

"Tuul was my last job to repay my debt to *The Cursed*. They saved me from my cousin over a year ago. My fiancée sold me out. My black market merchant dealings were too much tarnish for her upper class image."

She dropped the piece of fabric into the basin, shocked more than anything and angry she hadn't take some skin or an ear from the spiteful trollop when she'd boarded the ship seeking Ian's help.

He continued. "I owed them, and I couldn't pay in coin…. All my assets had been seized and turned over to my bastard relation. I paid them for their favor in jobs. Bounty hunting, stealing, intelligence retrieval, whatever they needed. One last deal and I was done."

Then numbness hit when she saw his frustrated expression as he scrubbed the beginnings of facial hair on his cheeks. Somehow, over the weeks of travel, companionship, and the sharing of a bed and bodies, she'd begun to believe they were on the same side. His words said another story, one she didn't believe wholeheartedly. Another fact…. "You lied to me."

"I didn't lie. I never got the chance to tell you because you never asked; you assumed."

She scoffed and turned to face him. Better to take the punch to the face than a knife to the back. "Really? Any chance is a good one. Maybe before you took me to bed or when I told you my sordid past?"

"Oh, it's not like you've shared all your secrets.

145

Who you are is the only one. Why *The Cursed*? Why Luther? Don't think I missed the bloodlust in your eyes when Eva and I discussed him. You're desperate to find them, desperate enough to bring a man on board you had vowed to kill."

She threw her hands in the air. Then she put both hands against his chest and shoved. "Don't talk about things you know nothing about."

He barely moved two steps. "Then tell me about them. Confess, Sorella. The number of lives you've taken means nothing, but what does?"

"My brother!"

His mouth dropped, hard gaze softening.

Anger, revenge, justice, and killing, she dealt with almost daily. But pity? That was one thing she had never handled well. She stalked over to the porthole, staring out into the hazy gray sky, a reminder of how horrible the day had turned out to be, a reminder of how lines were blurring now.

"I was six, and they kidnapped me. He was given in my stead as the ransom. A twelve year-old trained bodyguard, my bodyguard. We were very close."

"So it's revenge." He stood only a few steps behind her, speaking softly.

"Yes…. no…. I don't know, but I want to find him. We were meant to follow orders, but I couldn't forget him. My parents didn't forget to remind me, either, of his sacrifice for my future. How it was so important to live up to my potential."

"As a killer?"

"That's wrong, isn't it?" She'd lost sight of any moral line. She'd betrayed her family, but for reasons of her own making. At the same time, she had never

146

seen her parents as horrible people, just people who were fighting for what they believed in. Their only mistake was giving up her brother.

"It's wrong to trade human lives or expect someone to kill because you say so," he said, coming closer now. He wrapped his arms around her, and she melted into his embrace. Not the best path to take, but she needed the comfort—such a foreign thing, but she'd easily become addicted to it.

"Yet you were trading Tuul for your life." The irony wasn't lost on her.

"I'm afraid you're wrong. I wasn't trading his life to them, merely his services. I've never known Luther to actually sell people."

She laughed then, attempting to pull away from him, but no dice. "We'll have to beg to differ. Nearly every crewman on board this ship has lost a relative to *The Cursed* and their slave trade. Disappearing acts, one and all. Can't even track them."

"Hey." He nipped the lobe of her ear, awakening the part of her that still wanted him, needed him in a physical way. "I'm not saying they don't. I'm saying I haven't seen it happen."

They stood, staring out the porthole, watching a flock of birds fly by. Before retiring, Sorella had pointed the helmsman in the direction of a small group of islands where they'd dock and repair before venturing toward Luther's hiding place. She still planned on taking *The Cursed* out, but first she needed to determine a few things. Ian rubbed her shoulders with his hands, kneading her flesh to a state of relaxation she'd never experienced.

"I'm sorry," she confessed, not wanting their

intimacy to end and sensing in him a true fear of the repercussions of her actions. Sure, instinct told her Gretchen would've met death if she'd let things play out, and, truth be told, trusting someone else to manage a dangerous situation like that seemed nigh impossible. Still, guilt ate at her, and thoughts of how the outcome could've been changed were taking root in her mind.

"For what?" He tucked his head next to hers, resting his chin on her shoulder.

"For killing Tuul, for hiding things, for being me."

"But I like you, and I'm sorry for not telling you what I was getting in return for the bounty. At first, I thought if I told you, you'd kill me."

"I would've," she murmured. Now…. Never.

He chuckled, a few feather light kisses from his lips touching the side of her neck. "See, you're good at this honesty thing."

"Then let's be honest. What will Luther accept in Tuul's stead?"

His arms loosened, hands grabbing her shoulders and turning her to face him. "What are you thinking?"

"You give him someone more valuable."

"Who knows how valuable the man I already had was? I don't know what he was wanted for."

"Still, I've got someone in mind who is much more valuable than Tuul could ever be." She smiled, a plan unfurling from her rampant thoughts.

Ian's eyes narrowed, suspicious, and she flashed a full grin. "No." He shook his head. "Absolutely not. Having me deliver you to him is the worst idea ever."

"It'd get me close enough to kill him without a fight."

148

"Will it bring your brother back?" He stepped in close again, resting his forehead against hers and lighting flames of desire and frustration along the way.

"I don't care. Retribution for a life." Her words came out labored as he started unfastening the buttons on her vest. Allowing him access to her body had been a mistake if she failed to control herself. She struggled to maintain coherent thoughts, to pay attention as he spoke again.

"Why such extremes when questions may yield different results?" He kissed her nose, and her eyes closed. Then he slid her vest off and tossed it to the side, her balisongs rattling in their holsters when they hit the floor. "Why inflict death when you've experienced the very act that produces life?"

"Oh," she moaned when his hands cupped her breasts. Her mouth hungrily wanted his, but, instead, he sucked one of her nipples into his mouth. "You're trying to convince me that killing isn't worth it?"

He lifted his head and returned to the gentle, tender pressing of his lips on her eyelids, cheeks, and finally her mouth. "I'm just saying explore other options, and then, if needed, respond with force."

"Where did they teach you the art of diplomacy?" She allowed herself to look at him then, to be 'open,' as Bonita often described their talks.

"In ballrooms, store fronts, and dinner parties across N'awlins'," he grinned at her as his voice dropped into the southern, French-tinted accent she'd heard in Janken's club, "I learned the best way to survive is to refrain from the horrible practices of the dictators you wish to depose."

"I mean to depose no one." She stepped back, then, away from kisses and erotic daydreams.

"You were trained to be someone who eliminated people and obstacles. My president is as much a tyrant as the kaiser."

"Yes, but I ran away so I wouldn't have to kill him." She kept backing away from him, traversing the room until her back lined up with the cabin door.

"Oh, isn't ridding the world of *The Cursed* the same thing, except this time it's on your own agenda? The blight of the German Empire and the United States wiped out by a weapon of their own making?"

The words were cruel, sharp, and cut like the very knives she'd trained with for the last ten years. Cold reality replaced tender feelings, and she hated it, despised the pity in his gaze mixed with an emotion she failed to recognize. "I think you need to leave." Her hand found the doorknob behind her.

"Sorella, I—"

"No, you've said enough. I've become what they made me, what they intended me to be. Only this time, I'm killing their enemies for them, right?" She couldn't bring herself to twist the knob as if turning it would plunge a knife completely into her heart. This man made her weak, awaking emotions in her she didn't want to experience. Emotions made her care what he thought of her and how she appeared. He even made her care for the well-being of people she wasn't responsible for.

"You're not what they want you to be yet. There's a fine line. All I'm saying is why kill at all? It proves nothing. Gives nothing."

She thought about the deaths she'd caused. Two

recent ones gave her nothing but peace because the little girl who would've been hurt was spared instead. Other deaths were meant as messages or occurred as self-defense. In some cases, she'd been able to disarm rather than slay or inflict enough pain to cause surrender, but it had always been simpler to destroy her enemies or problems. "It's easier."

"That's why you do it?"

"Yes." Honesty served as a painful companion. "And in rare cases, necessary."

"Rare, meaning…"

"When someone has a gun trained on your head and won't hesitate to shoot." The image of the German soldier's gun pointed at Ian flashed in her mind, one image she'd prefer to never see again.

"Valid point." He approached her cautiously, much like the first night he'd kissed her, no doubt afraid she'd rebuke him. Her hand still clasped the doorknob firmly. It was a lifeline, a way to remove his threat to her emotional stability. This man truly brought out the worst feelings, yet he proved wise, brave, and downright irresistible when it came to seduction.

"Now you should—"

He reached her, putting a single finger up to her lips. "Wait one minute. Let me say this last thing, and then you can kick me out, stab me, or whatever you want." He looked upward as if the ceiling could assist him in finding the words to say. "I'm sorry for my harsh words and for the teasing. If you'll let me, I'll make it up to you. If not, I'll respect your wishes."

"Why say the words, then, and do all of this?" She shoved him, righteous anger restored. This time he gave, moving back two steps. Another shove and another step.

"I wanted you to see what I see. To see what you're capable of."

"And what's that?" she growled.

"Compassion. Empathy."

Ian gave a small smile as her eyebrows lifted from their narrowed position, and her jaw fell open.

Since she'd entered the cabin, he'd run through his own whirlwind of feelings, highs to lows and back again. From anger to love…. *Love, hell.* Each time he'd attempted sympathy, she'd stir him up again, only to have him fall as soon as he extracted another verbal dissection from her. This time, he couldn't tell if she planned on hitting him or embracing him. Instead, she crumpled to the floor, her physical actions mirroring how he felt—drained.

He dropped with her, pulling her into his arms as she sobbed. To see her cry broke his heart. This was never his intention, no matter how frustrated or confused he found himself. An ache took residence in his chest, something dull and throbbing like he'd been hit with a heavy punch. Maybe, just maybe, words would soothe his pain as well as hers.

"I'm sorry. I'm sorry." He continued murmuring apologies, lips pressed against her hair, breathing in the scent of gardenia amidst the smells of cleaning solutions. No doubt she'd scrubbed up the blood and mess alongside her crew while he'd sat in her room, sulking like a child.

"I didn't want to see. It hurts…. All this hurts." She clung to him, hands fisting his shirt.

When did things become complicated? *The minute I set foot on this ship.* Too true because he had found himself wrapped up in her sarcasm, her biting retorts, and even the way she threw a knife. He was fascinated at how, one minute, she was the most dangerous person he'd ever met, and, in the next, a lady who danced like an angel. He'd make it up to her.

"Let me take the hurt away."

"How?" She looked up then, cheeks streaked with water tracks.

"With this," he said before fusing his mouth to hers.

Instead of pushing away, she pulled him closer, biting at his lips then soothing them with licks of her tongue as if trying to mete out a punishment of sorts and a very enticing penance at that. Giving her control over the embrace, he grew hard as the kiss deepened.

She rose onto her knees, hands moving to his shirt and ripping it open, then pushing the cotton fabric along with his jacket off his shoulders and onto the floor. With his chest bared, their mouths still battled, breaking every few seconds as she removed her own shirt.

He heard more than saw the rustling, felt the movement of her arms as they brushed his chest. Then her bare skin slid against his and he lost his mind. Standing up, he broke their embrace and tugged her with him, lifting her into his arms and marching toward the bed. He threw her onto the mattress, loving the sound she made, a delighted noise, when she landed.

As he shed his boots and pants, she watched, licking her lips and driving him wild. "Take off the rest," he said. Not a suggestion—no, a demand, which she obeyed.

In less than a minute, she lay there without a stitch of clothing covering her, naked, gooseflesh pebbling her skin.

"Are you cold?"

She nodded.

He joined her on the bed, covering her with his body. "Then let me light you on fire."

They kissed, the motions ravenous, needy. Her fingers raked his flesh then gripped him at the wrists, the restraint enflaming him as much as everything else she did.

Between embraces, she mumbled, "Let me on top."

"Happy to oblige as soon as I taste you." He moved down her body, still allowing her to hold him captive, and she spread her legs in invitation. Moisture glistened on her folds like a beckoning call. He lowered his tongue to lap at her, unable to do anything with his hands. Somehow the inability to touch her with anything besides his mouth turned him on even more.

Her eyes rolled backward as he began a fresh assault, flicking her clit with multiple strikes then plunging into her, mimicking the very action he planned to take with another part of him soon. She moaned and tugged on his arms. He went with the motion, slipping his tongue from her, dragging against the sensitized flesh until he stopped at her hood and sucked her clitoris.

"Ian," she cried out.

No relenting, no holding back; he kept sucking, using his teeth to nibble at her. He'd wanted to make her scream, and she did, her release coming with her verbal declaration. Then his arms were free. He hoisted her by wrapping one arm under each thigh and lifting her halfway off the bed, mouth still on her pussy as he lapped up her orgasm, the taste of her something he'd never get enough of. Tangy but sweet, this flavor was a fine delicacy one could only get at the juncture between her thighs.

Her chest heaved as he removed her limbs from his shoulders and gently put her back on the bed. "Your turn," she said, dragging herself to her knees and motioning for him to lie down. Her gaze was sharp, nothing like the drugged, sensual look of a woman in the aftermath of pleasure.

He lay back against the pillows, worried her devious expression hinted at a joke he didn't know. She gripped his cock; it pulsed in her hand as she held it, her long, tanned fingers a sharp contrast against his pink flesh.

Lowering her head, she swiped the tip with her tongue. Feeling wet heat against his flesh, he naturally rocked his hips upward, wanting the cocoon she teased him with. A little idiot voice inside his head reminded him she'd never done this before. Bastard that he was, he liked the idea of being her first in all things. He'd already taken her maidenhead; no hardship to let her allow him another guilty pleasure.

So he forced himself to relax, letting his body release the tension taking hold as she wrapped her lips around his cock. Heaven offered no sweeter place than this room or the tongue swirling around his length. Soon she began moving up and down, finding a rhythm, and his legs tensed, feet arching as she cupped his balls.

Holy hell. He didn't want to come yet. He wanted to feel her slick heat first. "Stop."

She did as he asked. "Is something wrong?"

"No, but I want you to ride me like you wanted, and if you keep doing that, I'll be out for a bit."

Smiling she let go and straddled him. Taking him in hand once more, she guided his cock to her entrance. As he slid in, she gasped.

"Okay?"

"Mmhmm," she moaned, impaling herself on him. He nearly came then, watching the look of abandon on her face. She reached up and touched her nipples, squeezing them between thumbs and index fingers.

Her hips gyrated, grinding her inner walls against his member. She moved up and down in slow, mind-numbing movements meant to prolong the torment. Some tender emotion snagged his heart in the midst of the most sensual experience of his life as she moaned, "Ian."

He needed to grab control, to wrestle the beast in him into submission through climax. Grabbing her hips, he moved her in a fast-paced, pounding race to the finish line, only to pull her forward and off his cock at the last second squirting his come onto her back. "I'm sorry."

"For what?" she asked, wiping a bead of sweat from his forehead and licking it with her tongue. Hell, this woman amazed him time and again.

"Not giving you another orgasm."

"Well, it's not over yet, is it?" She gave him a wicked grin.

Most likely she'd be the death of him, but until then, he'd give anything to please her for as long as she'd have him. "No, my captain, indeed, it's not."

Chapter Fifteen

They stayed in bed all afternoon, loving each other. The only time she rose from the bed was to acknowledge Bastille and give him directions for repairs as they docked at the town of Torshavn in the Faroe Islands. Then back to Ian's arms, she went, making love multiple times as the sinking sun faded. Some sessions were rough, and others were sweet, tender…as if Ian wanted to wash away her previous sins by loving her body as thoroughly as possible.

After the sun set, she fell asleep and woke to grapes being dangled in front of her face. "I brought food," he said, plucking one of the fruits from the vine and pushing it between her lips. She bit into the tart, sweet orb, loving the taste as it exploded in her mouth.

"Where did you get them?"

"Bonita and her fancy speech gained a whole crate from a merchant in the harbor. He'd brought them north from Greece to sell to someone interested in trying their hand at wine making, but the buyer was late to show."

She grabbed a grape from the vine herself. "Our luck, then."

"Indeed. I've also got hot soup and bread if I can tempt you from the beneath the covers to eat with me." He leaned back, letting her see the spread he'd assembled for them. How she'd slept through the noise, she didn't know. She'd become less cautious with this man around. Her training usually had her awake at the slightest movement.

Her stomach grumbled.

"Obviously, you're hungry."

"I could eat." She threw the covers back, presenting her naked body to the cold air. Her nipples tightened at his eager perusal.

"Maybe waiting a little while isn't a bad idea."

She wagged her finger at him. "No. We wouldn't want the soup to go cold."

"You're right. Food first, pleasure later."

He moved away, placing the fruit back on the table and gathering a robe for her from the dressing screen. No additional ogling granted, she donned the proffered robe, tying a neat bow at her waist, and rose to join him. Two chairs with pillows on the seats provided comfortable seating, and steam wafted from the bowls placed at each setting. A spoon, a knife, half a loaf of bread, and the rest of the grapes completed their fare.

"Drink?" she asked.

"Ah, yes." He reached to the side of the table, disappearing for a moment and then emerging with a bottle of wine and two glasses. "A little Madeira also courtesy of Bonita's fine negotiating tactics."

Popping the cork, he poured a little into his glass and tasted it first. Whether he was checking for poison or taste, she didn't know, but appreciated the gesture. "Perfect."

Filling the glasses halfway, he handed one to her. "A toast," he announced, raising the glass. "To a beautiful dinner companion, delicious food, and a cook I'll need to steal after we meet with *The Cursed*."

She smiled and clinked her glass against his before taking a healthy swallow. "Would you really try to steal her?"

"The woman knows her bartering skills. She was a force to be reckoned with on the dock. When I'm in the merchant world again, a woman like that would be a leg up from the help I'm used to getting."

"Where are you getting your help from?" She took a sip of the soup, potatoes in cream broth with onions and other vegetables. No meat, but such a commodity would be scarce anywhere in Europe, and on a small chain of islands, non-existent.

"The streets mostly. I tried to give young boys and girls a chance to get out of the future already set up for them and away from parents who'd sell their bodies or trade slave labor for drugs. It's bad in my hometown, but I'm sure you've seen plenty of places like those in Europe."

Tearing a piece of bread from the loaf, she shook her head. "No, surprisingly, people in Europe value their children. More often those children are eager to work or join the kaiser's army as a means to ensure their family's safety. That's how he's winning, offering food, clothing, and the promise of more." She dipped the bread into her soup. "When you're starving, you'll give anything to ensure your belly stays full. I've seen men and women who were determined to refuse, give in as soon as the cupboards are bare."

Taking a bite from her bread, she looked up. His face was filled with anguish. "He needs to be stopped. Germany needs to be stopped."

"Why?" she asked between bites. "Because they're

smarter at war and winning over the starving masses with flour?"

Ian scoffed. "No, they need to be stopped because what they are doing is wrong. You know it, and you hate it as much as I do. Yet you hide behind a mask of indifference."

"I don't hide. I choose to remove myself from the conflict. As you so eloquently put it on the floor of the Embassy, live one day at a time with what happiness you can make for yourself."

The frown he wore deepened.

"I'll admit this conversation is making the dinner less happy by the second," she said.

"I'm sorry." He reached for her hand, threading their fingers together. "Let's discuss other things. The repairs on the ship are finished, and Bastille wanted me to tell you we can depart whenever you wish."

A rock of indecision lodged in her belly. Leaving meant going after *The Cursed* and the possibility she'd lose Ian. Instead of formulating a plan, she'd spent all day in his arms. Now she hadn't the faintest idea what to do besides fly up and offer herself in his place, for his debt to be absolved.

"Sorella, what's wrong?"

He must've caught her frown. She gave a little laugh. "Just thinking how awful it will be to not have any more grapes after today. I'm sure the crew is enjoying the treat."

"They are...." The last word dragged out as he let go of her and went back to his meal. "You can speak freely, you know."

"I want to send scouts ahead to survey *The Cursed* hideout."

"That's not really necessary—"

She didn't care, but it would buy time. "Humor me. I'm not suggesting because I plan to attack, merely as a safety precaution. We just got into an air battle over your bounty, which I killed. I want to make sure Luther isn't prepping to come after me once he receives the bad news."

The nod he gave seemed half-hearted.

"What?"

"It'd be better to just fly in. Announce yourself, and let him welcome you."

Now it was her turn to make an unladylike snort. "And you really think he will?"

"I've seen him do the same for countless airships."

"No doubt his mercenary partners." The gang had to be well connected with a large number of airships to move as they did and receive information.

He patted the back of her hand. "Then why not pretend you want to become one. A banner of truce will get you invited in. Whatever you decide, to attack or not, you won't have to sneak around or endanger crew members." The suggestion held merit, more than she would like to openly admit.

Another thing she refused to admit, at least out loud, was that she really wanted to stay in port for another day and continue her tryst with Ian. If she couldn't confess her feelings to him, though, it was time to start planning their approach to *The Cursed*. She swallowed another spoonful of soup, letting the silence drag out.

"So do you like my idea?" He was positively yummy when feisty, teeth clenched and impatient.

"It's not horrible. Have any others?"

He watched his captain talk with Bastille, watched her explain the plan to the helmsman, and even watched her walk and whisper to each crewman on deck. He was lost. No matter how much she infuriated him or attempted to argue with him, he wanted her. The logic he'd so poetically quoted to her about sex not equaling emotion was officially thrown in his face.

The truth was he'd been hooked since the moment she'd stabbed the dirty bastard who'd wanted to hurt Gretchen; since she'd danced with him on the deck of the ship, and then in a ballroom where all her secrets were on display. He loved her. Such a pesky word, love, but like his memories of yesterday, it shoved its way to the forefront of his mind, wedging itself in with his moral compass.

Now they were almost to *The Cursed's* island, maybe a half hour away. He'd stayed up late with Sorella, planning how they'd handle their arrival and the upcoming talk with Luther. Then he'd held her, made love to her, possessed her at first in a sweet, caring way, but things quickly turned heated and frenzied at her insistence, as if they couldn't get close enough, as if time slipped away from them. The more passionate the lovemaking, the more likely they'd bind their souls together.

Hell. Binding souls? He'd lost his mind, yet in the confusion, he'd made a decision. No sense in trading her secrets for his freedom. No, he'd take another job; blame Tuul's death on the invading bounty hunters. No one knew differently except for him, Bonita, Bastille, and Gretchen.

Then if she'd have him, escort him aboard the *Liberté* on this last job, they'd soon be together…free.

She approached him as he stood, back to the wall, one booted foot propped against the steel and planking. "Are you ready?"

"As I'll ever be. Does everyone know the plan?"

She nodded, reaching behind him to spin his spur with her finger. "Why the spurs?"

"An American pastime I was always fascinated with. The cowboys of the Midwest used these to help control their horses when riding, but I like them for the sound they make."

"Interesting. I never learned much about cowboys. They mainly taught me about the president, his household, your country's customs, and their expectations of me." She took a spot beside him and nudged him with her shoulder. "Tell me something else. Something interesting."

He wanted to tell her he loved her, to tell her he'd be ensuring they both got out of there today with her secrets intact. Instead, he told her, "I met the president's son once."

"You did?" She sounded genuinely shocked.

"My father was one of the richest landowners in the entire parish. Roosevelt's son went on a tour of the States and wanted to stop in New Orleans. He likes jazz music, as I'm sure you know."

She smiled. "I didn't know. You'd be surprised at the lack of information we've been given about him over the years. At our first introduction, he barely said anything to me even while we danced. He looked at my bosom plenty and gave me a few polite comments about my dress and how he was looking forward to getting to know me better."

Ian clenched his fists at the idea of the leering Roosevelt Jr. touching his captain. At least he could boast being her first in everything physical, not that pervert. "Trust me when I say the last thing he wants is purity. He has some deplorable tastes. When he visited my parish, he wanted to know the whereabouts of the brothels in town. In a crunch, people would come to me looking for anything and everything, and so did he. That's the only reason I know about it."

"Thank goodness I got out of that situation then. I'd have killed him when I found out."

Surprising how serious she was on the topic. Loveless marriages were no doubt something she'd become familiar with. He chuckled.

"What?"

"You're committed to monogamy?" What he really wanted to know was if she'd be committed to such a thing with him, a thought too dangerous to say out loud and not at all appropriate.

"If I pledged my future to someone, I'd expect him to be only with me. I've seen relationships without love or care between the spouses. I don't want that."

How the hell had he let himself get involved in this type of conversation? Yet not asking the next logical question seemed to be impossible. "Do you plan on getting married someday?"

Sorella froze like a mouse caught in the open. She stammered. "I...uh, that is—"

Not a hard question in his mind, but she was still struggling with her answer when the helmsman called out, "Land Ho!"

In the distance, the isle of Grimsey loomed, small, serviceable, with three other airships ported, from what Ian could make out. He left his post against the wall and headed for the railing. The island looked like a large boat in the ocean. He found himself surprised Luther could house his operations from such a location.

"Fifteen minutes until docking time. Do you want to run through the plans again…in private?" Sorella said, stroking the side of his arm with one hand.

"You're insatiable."

"Take happiness when you can, you've said as much before. Who knows what the day will bring?"

He looked down at her, needing to reconfirm just one thing. "You'll let me take the lead, right? Luther will be comfortable with me. I'll ease you into the conversation. This won't work any other way."

She nodded. "You've got the lead unless I receive a sign from you or Bastille telling me something's wrong."

"Nothing will go wrong." If it did, they'd be in for the fight of their lives, and the last thing he wanted to do was harm Sorella and her crew. At worst, he'd have her leave if *The Cursed* leader refused to hear him out. "Tell your helmsman to port next to Luther's main ship on the west side of the island. Most likely, he's there. If not, his first mate will point us in the right direction."

She stalked off, probably upset at him for not taking advantage of a quick coupling behind closed doors, but he needed to keep his wits intact. Her body, in all its tantalizing glory, did the exact opposite. If things went as he hoped, he'd be wrapped up in her body for as long as possible. Waiting a few hours wouldn't hurt.

***

A swarm of moths took root in her belly, fluttering like mad as the docking rope was let loose and secured by her crewman at the post on the island. *The Cursed* flag ship, a massive beast bigger than hers and fully outfitted with EMP repel netting, docked to their right. Did this gang's leader know where her brother was?

Nerves, excitement, anxiety…. Damn him for not taking her mind off things with a mindless screw. She'd needed something to distract her, but didn't want to appear weak. Her crew had to see her as strong, impervious to emotion. Sentiment was only allowed for her men.

She'd led them in the past with strong actions. Confused by her order to stay the attack in favor of parlay, many had expressed their concerns earlier today, but they were willing to follow her lead.

Finding another way to get her men the justice they wanted would be difficult. Most were like her. Next to gold, they saw blood as the currency to repay all debts. She hoped Ian was right, and that, somehow, the worst things she'd heard about Luther weren't true, but merely lies spread by *The Cursed's* enemies, much like the propaganda spread by the kaiser and his cronies to brainwash the weak.

As Ian stood on the deck of the *Liberté,* waving a white flag made from some cloth Bonita had provided, *The Cursed's* gangplank extended from their ship, crossing the air to join Sorella's in an invitation. Once the narrow metal path reached her gate's opening, the crew set about securing it for crossing.

Small metal tips were put over the front of Ian's shoes. Having already applied hers, Sorella hastened from the helm's deck to his side.

"Ready?" he asked, smiling as if their conversation minutes before, his dismissal of her advances, had never taken place. She loved the look in his eyes, his genuine caring for her well-being, and immediately her worry lightened, her unwarranted anger replaced with a foreign emotion, one she'd dismissed before. But the time for analyzing personal feelings would have to await the completion of their mission, the attainment of their goal. She'd shove them aside like everything else and focus on the task at hand.

"Let's do this."

The tips on their boots kept them magnetized to the gangplank. The air brisk, Sorella whipped the sides of her coat around her. She'd worn the trench and her vest. All three balisongs were on her person with an extra stashed in her boot, followed by a much larger knife in the trench coat's inside pocket. They had decided on no guns the night before, but he'd winked when she'd responded that she wouldn't travel into unknown territory without her blades.

Even with magnetized tips, the walk could still be dangerous, and they took each step slowly, planting one foot firmly before moving the next. She had a habit of attempting to slide her boot after putting it in place to make sure the magnet held. No harm in double checking.

At last they reached the other side, her lover boarding the ship first. She followed, and Bastille brought up the rear.

"Any weapons?" a man with a grizzled chin barked at her.

"Besides this boot and my hands? No."

He didn't like her response and pointed a rifle at her. "Open the coat."

Ian stepped between them. "There's no need. I briefed her on protocol."

"I don't care if you felt her up before crossing the bridge way, she'll open the coat," the rifleman replied.

She tapped her well-intentioned protector on the shoulder, and he stepped aside. "Where I come from, men have better manners." Spreading her coat flaps, she showed him her fully clothed form.

"In my experience, anyone can kill, lady." He reached forward and pulled out her big knife. "What do you use this for…eating?"

"Yes, and what I eat is my personal business." She wagged her eyebrows to imply whatever horrible thing his imagination brought up.

The rifleman tossed the blade to a compatriot and moved on to Bastille. A quick pat down yielded no results. "Your weapon will stay with us until you're ready to leave. Proceed to the main cabin. Do you need directions?" His sarcastic tone revealed his opinion of them.

"I know where it is," Ian replied, stalking forward.

If things did go wrong, she'd enjoy torturing that one. She smiled a full grin, and her blackened teeth did the job for her. He flinched.

Ian's spurs clinked against the deck like a steady beat to their doom. When he opened the door to the main cabin and walked inside, a loud, booming, happy voice cried out, "Merchant, you bastard. Where the hell have you been? I expected you a week ago."

"Things didn't go quite as planned, Luther."

Her pulse raced. The man she'd been hunting stood on the other side of a wood and metal door. Without thinking, her hand went to a balisong pocket. *It'd be easy to let the thing fly.* She'd already triangulated his location in the room based on Ian's gaze and his voice. *It would be so simple to end the whole thing.*

Except that the man who had ensnared her heart reached back and put a hand on hers. He tugged it away from her weapon and wrapped it up in his own warmth. His reassuring gaze said all would be well.

"Hit a few snags. Nothing I couldn't handle," Ian said.

"Good to hear. The boys were starting to call you a lightweight, especially Roscoe over here. Doesn't think anyone's capable of getting things done."

Ian pulled her forward through the door and into the room. "Yes, I got lucky, thanks to a lovely captain and her crew. Allow me to introduce her."

She glanced first at the number of bodies. Three men, one behind a desk with two others flanking him. Books, maps, and nailed documents lined the walls. The leader must be a busy and methodical man to keep such close records. Even Sorella didn't monitor things that closely.

Then she looked at Luther, finding his ebony eyes locked on hers. Chin and head covered in hair black as the smoke from the kaiser's industrial factories, he wore leather over a grimy white shirt and gnawed on an unlit cigar, but the hoops hanging in both ear lobes were familiar. The scar running down his left cheek— a mirror to the one her brother had received when he'd interfered with one of her training sessions.

"Friend, this is Captain—"

The cigar dropped. "Sorella?" The mercenary's eyes went soft. He shoved himself out of the chair and bustled over to her.

She struggled for her blade, pulling her hand free from Ian's and reaching for it. He wasn't who she thought he was. Couldn't be. As she flicked the balisong open, Luther knocked it out of her hand. She readied for attack, completely unprepared when he grabbed her in his big, meaty arms and bundled her up in a hug, squeezing her tight. "Sister," he cried, the word slightly muffled since his face was smashed against her headscarf.

"Sette?"

Chapter Sixteen

Ian looked at Bastille, and the first mate's confused expression mirrored his. "Who's Sette?" His question came out as Luther placed Sorella back on the ground and let her go.

"I am," the large leader replied. "I changed my name years ago. Less conspicuous since I didn't want the people I worked with to know I was Italian."

"But they ransomed you." His captain's voice cracked again. Tears welled in her eyes.

"No time too spring a leak, little sister. They did ransom me, and I became indispensable for *The Cursed*'s head. My skills with numbers, not to mention weapons, has kept me alive all this time. When the last leader died, I took over, but instituted a few changes."

This was a better outcome than anything Ian had expected. Yet his captain had hijacked the entire proceeding. Probably best to step back, stay quiet, and let the two siblings get reacquainted.

"Changes?" Sorella's voice was heavy with suspicion.

The mercenary laughed. "Sit down, and I'll tell you. Roscoe, get drinks for everyone."

She took a seat, and Ian grabbed a chair next to hers. Their host resumed his spot behind the desk. Ironic that Bastille took a position against the far wall, his eyes on the door. Probably where he felt the most comfortable.

"Sister, despite the rumors, we are a revolutionary

group. I've been leading a private war against the kaiser for years. Even now, I'm gathering new information that will reveal some of his future plans."

She leaned forward in her seat, hands gripping the arms of the chair. "What about stealing people?"

"I haven't stolen anyone. The last person to be stolen was a boy, and he's now a well-trained spy."

"My crew would beg to differ. Members of their family went missing, and all claim to have tangled with *Cursed* members."

Both Ian's friend and his captain frowned. Frustration filled the room until Roscoe burst in with a tray containing a pot of tea and a bottle of brandy. "Wasn't sure what ya'd be thirsty fo'," he announced, shoving the tray onto the desk. Cups rattled, and liquid sloshed.

"The family members?" She inquired again, and Ian wondered if maybe his earlier thoughts would prove wrong, if reunited siblings would shed blood.

Luther poured himself a glass of brandy and motioned a half-filled glass toward Ian. He reached for it and sat back. Sorella stared at him, narrow-eyed. He'd beg forgiveness if they survived this, but he wouldn't refuse a stiff drink. The revelations of the last few minutes required liquid fortitude, and if she deemed it consorting with the enemy…. *Oh, well.*

"Everyone I've saved is safe at my facility in Iceland. They were taken for their knowledge, their skills, or because the secret police and inspectors would've grabbed them sooner or later. I don't keep anyone who says they want out, but no one wants out. I provide them opportunities of a lifetime."

"I don't believe you."

173

Ian didn't believe him either. The island country was fairly populated and remained independent of Europe by vowing to remain neutral. It also had little to no resources to offer Germany's power hungry dictator. "Why would they risk their non-aggressor status to hide you?"

"Et tu, Brute?" Luther didn't look offended despite his off-hand Shakespearean remark. Hell, he winked at them. "I pay them a lot of money and keep certain items, normally unavailable, flowing into their markets freely. Pigs, goats, and sheep go a long way to opening previously closed doors. I don't demand their loyalty for it, merely a place to base my refugees."

Sorella scoffed. "I still don't believe you."

"Little sister, do you trust your first mate?"

She looked back at Bastille, who nodded at her. "With my life. He replaced you as body guard, big brother. We've been friends for many years."

"Ah…. Then why not let him take the *Liberté*, your crew, and my man, Roscoe, to the mainland and go to the camp. Your crewmates can reunite with their loved ones, and you'll have your proof."

Ian saw the skepticism on her face. He prayed she'd give the idea a shot. They hadn't even gotten to the really bad news yet, the subject probably on the tip of Luther's tongue once this first issue was resolved.

"Fine, but they have to return in precisely two hours, or I'll cut your damn head off." His captain's promise had the other guards grabbing at their coil guns.

Luther raised his hands. "Relax, men. She won't

try anything right now. Just a promise for future retribution, which I can respect. Be gone, Roscoe. Show my sister's man where the camp is, but watch the time closely."

The two large men marched out the door at Luther's command, Bastille taking up the rear. The *Liberté's* first mate cast one last glance at Ian and gave another nod. That heavy lidded gaze told him he'd be held responsible for Sorella's safety if, for some reason, she died, and he didn't.

Once the door shut, Luther trained eyes, black beady eyes, resembling a raven staring down a dying animal, on him "Now, where's my bounty?"

Being on the offensive came easy to Sorella, especially since her brother looked so different and she still had difficulty reconciling his grown-up face to the boy she knew. Then he'd offered everything tidy and tied up in a neat, perfect ending. Something rubbed her wrong about that.

When Luther, as he liked to be called, brought up the bounty, her stomach knotted like a tangle of ropes. They'd find out if dear brother still had his massive temper.

She copied her partner's easy demeanor, relaxing back into her arm chair and watching as he sipped from his brandy sifter. Maybe she should've taken a drink, too.

"About that. I'm afraid some other hunters killed him." The lie rolled out of Ian's mouth like jam spread on a biscuit, smooth and unwavering. *Damn him.* "They attacked the *Liberté*, demanded we turn over Tuul. Of course, you said it yourself; the mark was dangerous. The collar got damaged in an EMP attack. Once he was released, he went crazy, and got knifed in a scuffle. So I report to you empty handed and ready for another assignment."

This wasn't what they'd planned. The plan had involved him telling the truth, and then handing the conversation over to Sorella so she could offer herself and her skills in return for his freedom. Since the mercenary had revealed himself, she saw the solution plain as day. If the camp checked out, she'd work for him, and he'd release any hold he had on her lover's life.

Except Ian had gone off script.

"Wait, that's not—"

Luther waved his hand. "I don't care. What you're telling me is the one person who had a working knowledge of the kaiser's compound is *dead*. There's no one else, and it took me months to get the information I had. I sent you, Merchant, because you were the suave, slick merchant who could sell anyone on anything." As quick as he started speaking, he stopped. He changed to drumming his fingers on the desk. Then he quit nursing his alcohol and swallowed the rest in one gulp and turned to his sister. "Besides giving him a ride, what the hell are you here for?"

What an asshole. "Looking for you!" Sorella shoved out of her chair, slapping her palms on the top of the desk. "I've spent the last two years of my life searching for you, trying to find *The Cursed* so I could avenge you, only to find out you had become what I hoped you hadn't. And bounty hunters didn't kill your special bounty…. I did."

"Figures." Luther stood and pointed at Ian. "I've

got no more use for you. Too damn soft, and this job is about to get tough. You'll pay with your life."

She jumped in front of her lover, a gut reaction, screaming. "Stop! Please. Wait."

Gun fire sounded outside the cabin, bringing a halt to her outburst. She heard shots similar to those they had faced in Hamburg, but more of them.

Both men looked at each other, and each ran to separate portholes in the office. Instead of peeking out at the attack, she evaluated their situation inside. They had a few weapons, but all electric. If the boarders outside had an EMP, there'd be no chance at escape.

"Sister, why are there German soldiers storming my hideout?" Her brother's question came right before the EMP blast hit and the coil guns on the desk sputtered, then went dead. Too late.

Ian responded for her. "I have a feeling they somehow tracked us from Hamburg."

"You never thought to make sure no one was following you?"

Gripping two of her balisongs, Sorella swung them open. "We weren't followed in the traditional sense. My sensors never picked them up. If they tracked us, it's something new."

A loud whirr sounded, and Luther yelled, "Get down!" just as the door blew apart.

Ian dived on top of her, and they both hit the floor. Flying debris rained through the room. Then came a line of soldiers, rifles aimed. She heard the guns cock, and Ian pulled her to a standing position. Their arms went up, surrender preferable to death at the moment.

She heard some Deutsch hollered out at the back

of the line, but failed to make out the words clearly. The soldiers parted, letting someone important come to the forefront.

He appeared all in black with silver buttons lining his jacket and silver trim around his cuffs and neck. "Where is Herr Luther?"

"Here," her brother called out behind her. He stood behind the desk, broken cigar hanging from his mouth. "What the hell do you want, and why did you fire on my ship?"

"Ah, I sense hostility, though it's no surprise that a revolutionary such as yourself would be upset at men like me for doing my government's work. My name is Colonel Altenbach, and I'm here to place you and your associates under arrest."

Dread battled its way to the surface like a fish struggling against a river current, and Sorella fought to tamp it down. The *Liberté* was still out there, hopefully, but at this point, they had no back-up, no way to warn her crew that *The Cursed* ship was home to the enemy now.

"Come quietly, and we'll show leniency."

"What's that?" Ian quirked a brow.

The colonel smiled, a polite grin showing off a flawless set of teeth. "A quick death to you and all who oppose the kaiser."

"And if we aren't quiet?" Ian piped up with this question, still holding onto Sorella's arm.

"Oh, I don't expect you to be." Altenbach stepped up to them, reaching for her headscarf and snatching it off her head. "Especially during questioning."

***

178

Ian paced, and Sorella sat. It'd been at least a couple of hours since the colonel and his men had thrown them into their brig. Electrified bars greeted them like lost friends. He had never expected to end up in a cage.

Luther, the fearless leader, had been hauled away for the promised questioning, and Ian wondered if he'd give his sister up. That thought kept him moving and trying, in vain, to think constructively.

Both of them had already combed the compartment, looking for glitches in the technology and ways to short out the electricity, but with no luck. Two guards had been posted outside the cell, but they'd been called away. Now they reappeared with Ian's one-time friend nestled between them. Blood dripped from his chin, and one eye had already swollen shut.

One guard tapped the bars with an electo wand. A warning. Ian stepped away from the cell door. They threw their captive in shortly after, and though Ian rushed to help, his captain held back.

When the guards walked off again, Luther shoved him aside and pushed himself up to a standing position. "You were tracked." He spit, and blood hit the floor.

"What did they say?"

"Oh, nothing except you led them right to us. My dear sister's systems aren't very accurate after all."

Sorella's head came up, lips thinned.

Her brother moved toward her, and Ian stepped in front of him.

"Move out of my way," he growled, pointing a

finger at his sister. "You're spying for them, aren't you? They recruited you to get me. That's why you're not married."

Ian couldn't let her be degraded that way, so he responded, "No, she's been searching for you. Of all the lame-brained ideas —"

"Notice how she doesn't deny it."

He looked over at his lover, and she stared back at them, emotionless as ever and unassailable. Maybe her brother was right, and her acting skills rivaled all others. Suckered in by a woman again, but yet he'd taken her. She had submitted her virginity to him, rendering her impure in the eyes of the president's son.

"Maybe she's not speaking up because there's no sense arguing with someone who already thinks you're guilty?" He shoved Luther, pushing him half way back across the tiny space. "If she's a spy, why'd they leave her in here? She'd be in debrief already."

"You don't know how they work. I've seen it firsthand. Bastards sink their claws in so deep you'd never realize someone you love is corrupted to their cause until the very last minute." The words were filled with anguish. No doubt some of his mistrust came from Eva's actions.

"Or maybe your own woman betrayed you?"

Luther's head rose. "What the hell are you talking about?"

"Eva's the one who told us where you were. She also said that she wouldn't wait forever and we had to leave her behind. She could've cracked."

"Crooning whore!" A meaty fist slammed into the bars, the smell of singed flesh spreading through the air afterward. "I'll deal with her later. Now we have to get out of here."

"I have a plan."

Ian startled at the sound of Sorella's voice and the touch of her hand to his shoulder.

Her brother snorted. "Really?"

"It's time I turned myself in."

"Wächter!" Guard. A young man, all upper shoulders and chest, marched up to their cell followed by a second guard.

It was Ian's turn to grab Sorella, though his fingers were no real deterrent. If they wanted to get out of here, someone needed to be on the outside of the cage.

Sorella shrugged his hand way. *"Ich möchte den Altenbach sprechen."* *I want to talk to Altenbach.*

Another tap on the bars, another warning. She wouldn't try anything yet. The second soldier opened the cell door, and she stepped out. She glanced back into the cell one last time, meeting Ian's forlorn gaze. He was wondering, no doubt, where her loyalties lay. He'd find out soon enough if things went accordingly.

As they marched her to their superior, she counted stairs, soldiers, and guns, tucking each piece of information into her trained mind to hone a strategy. Unfortunately, to make things work she had to be taken all the way to the colonel, a better way to get a good read on all the potential pitfalls of attempting an escape. Maybe she could even convince the colonel to let them go.

The soldier prodding her along stopped in front of an office on the main deck. Then he motioned to another guard, who approached slowly, a pair of metal cuffs in hand.

"Give me your hands, *spinon*." Spy.

So they thought she worked for someone besides herself. How much fun would this be? She thrust both hands forward and relaxed as the ratchet clicked shut around each wrist. Obviously, they believed she was dangerous enough to warrant cuffs before meeting with their superior. She followed them through the door, taking note that the guard with the keys was to her left. Once inside, she was pushed into a plush black leather chair with silver studs lining its edges.

"*Guten Tag, Fraulein* Corvino." Altenbach leaned back in his chair, setting aside the documents he was looking over. Without his hat, the man's age was more evident. His blond hair was whitening at his temples in sharp contrast to a deep, red scar running along his hair line. "I've been expecting you."

"You have?"

"*Ja*. You want to trade yourself for your brother and partner, correct?"

She shook her head. "Not at all. I'm here to discuss the terms of your surrender."

He laughed then, a big, bawdy, throw-back-your-head laugh that echoed along the walls. "You're confident. I'll give you that, *Fraulein*. But what you see before you," he spread his arms wide, "is Tesla's latest accomplishment. Steel reinforced with rubber trim. EMP is no longer a problem with a ship such as this. So any type of attack you have planned won't work. You're better off surrendering your ship to us."

His monologue told her a lot of things, but more than anything, it gave her time to work loose the weapon she wore on her finger, a Bastille toy, containing the perfect amount of acid for the handcuffs. No doubt Ian would berate her later for using it here where she'd be in danger instead of at the cell door, but he was forgetting rule number one—know thy enemy.

Altenbach was too confident; too sure he'd won. His arrogance would ensure his downfall. A letter opener sat out on the desk, its metal blade glinting in the afternoon sunshine coming through a porthole. It dared her to use it—nay, it demanded she use it on her friendly colonel. He stood, turning his back to her, and clasped his hands behind him. *What a fool.* "Well, will you turn over your ship and return to serve the kaiser? I know your mother and father are anxious for word of your safe return, now that we've found you."

The top of the ring came off with ease, and she balanced it, slowly pouring the acid onto one cuff, and tilting to get it to move toward the lock. The chemical reaction immediate, bubbles rose from the surface. To cover the noise, she piped up, "You've heard from them then? My parents? They aren't angry?"

"How could they be angry? They were worried, worried you'd been killed by agents of our enemies. They are overjoyed, and already your mother has reached out to the president to inform him that his son's bride is almost done with her religious sabbatical."

She freed one hand and debated freeing the other. No time. Instead she rose from the chair and grabbed the letter opener. "That's good news. I was afraid of being deposed."

The next seconds were critical, but she moved, light as a feather, past the desk and slipped behind the colonel. Securing his hands with one of hers, she brought the sharp metal edge of the letter opener to his throat. "I won't be going back."

"Don't do—" His words were cut off, replaced with a gurgle as she slit the soft flesh, and blood poured out. He fell to the floor with a thump, and she backed away, taking up a position behind the door.

A few deep breaths and she was ready. The risks were great, and twenty men stood between her and the brig. Twenty bodies she'd have on her conscience until she recalled Ian's words, his reminder that she could accomplish all her goals without taking life. Who knew if these men had families that they were simply trying to feed by joining up in the kaiser's cause? To judge them by association.... She shook her head and cleared out the doubt, replacing it with resolve.

No matter what happened, she'd make it to her brother and Ian. She'd save them—without killing.

Chapter Seventeen

Gunfire sounded then shouts and yells. Ian stood and listened. Luther had taken up Sorella's spot, cursing quietly about not trusting women or family ever again.

"Be quiet," he hissed, trying to make out who the Germans were fighting. Possibly more of *The Cursed* mercenaries. Who knew? Regardless, the noises were getting closer; someone was coming for them.

When the brig door burst open, two guards fell backward, collapsing on the floor, expressions dazed. Then both guards let out moans of pain as Sorella stepped forward on top of them, pushing her boots into their abdomens with each step. The metal tips were still adhered, so no doubt those were biting into flesh through their uniforms.

"Are you both ready to get the hell out of here?"

He grinned. "Took you long enough."

"Says the man who's taking it easy while I disarm twenty men." She stepped up to the cell door and shoved a rubber key into the lock. "Once you're out, head to the top deck. Bastille and Roscoe are en route with the *Liberté*."

Luther grabbed Ian, shoving him out of the way, and stepping out of the cell first. "I'm not going anywhere. This ship has technology that would be useful. My men and I will commandeer it."

"For the mastermind of mercenaries, you're certainly not smart."

Brother and sister squared off, toe-to-toe.

"Really?"

"Yes, really. You have no idea if your men are dead or alive. We also don't know if more ships are on their way, and based on the conversation I just had with the colonel, these ships can't be tracked. Not in any way we know."

The mercenary laughed. "I'll be the judge of that. Get out of my way."

"You can't be serious."

Ian could let this play out, but instead he grabbed the electo wand from a fallen guard and moved into position. Dialing it took a bit longer than he had planned, and he was surprised at his captain's newfound patience. She'd never take the time to debate in the past, and he almost chuckled, thinking how he was acting more like her than she was.

Her brother nudged her aside with his arm, and that proved the perfect moment to strike. Stepping up, Ian touched the tip of the wand to his friend's back for five seconds. The look on the man's face was at first murderous then his features slumped. He crumpled in a heap on the floor.

"I can't believe you did that," Sorella marveled.

"What?" Ian leaned down to check Luther's pulse just to be on the safe side.

"You knocked him unconscious and spared me having to hurt him."

"Don't thank me yet. You'll have to help me drag him up to the next deck."

She helped him tug, pull, and manhandle her brother's body partially up the stairs. Luckily, Bastille popped up right as Sorella prepared to abandon the effort. The first mate helped Ian haul the big man up the half-flight of stairs. Getting him over to their ship proved a little more difficult, but after some creative thinking on Ian's part, they dropped him over the edge with the *Liberté* positioned right underneath.

"Where to next, my captain?" he asked as she finally came on board.

Between all available crew members, at least ten German soldiers were captured and shoved into the brig, the untrackable airship still tethered to *The Cursed* vessel.

"For now, we head to the mainland and stay on the lookout for more enemy vessels. I have no clue if they called for backup." Her braids hung loose, and she gathered each strand, entwining them at the back of her head. "And I'm not leaving until my asshole sibling promises not to harm you."

Funny, he'd expected her to be more worried about flesh and blood, the future of her crew, and the million other things they needed to concern themselves with, not his life. "We can worry about that later."

"No time like the present." Determination etched on her face, she pressed her lips together and marched off down the ship's hallway to do battle…for him.

She slammed open her cabin door. "Wake up, brother dear."

Luther was propped in a chair across from her desk, his hands and feet bound with thick rope. She circled him, and he sat up, scowling. "You'd better have a damn good reason for tying me up."

"We tied you up because you weren't showing

any."

"Who knocked me out?"

The question came as Ian slid into the room, shutting the door behind him. He kept near the exit though, watching them both.

"Never mind. Just untie me."

"I can't do that until you agree to cancel Ian's debt."

Luther laughed. "I'm afraid that's non-negotiable. You're a captain, and you know how it is. If they sense weakness, then you have to squash it like invading spiders. To let him go means I'm all right with people not delivering on their promises, not sticking to their word."

She knew, damn it. Her own words to Ian were similar. Success came with a price, and that meant empathy and compassion were traded away for a warm bed and food in the belly. She'd still had to fight for her life even after she'd escaped the ones attempting to control it.

Yet there were other options. Once thing she'd learned as a captain was to never give up. "How about a trade then?"

"You've got nothing."

"Not true." She pulled out one of her knives and stepped in front of him. "I've got your life in my hands, and if you'd don't give me Ian's life in exchange for yours, I'll show you exactly how I killed our German colonel."

"You've been arguing for him since the moment I said I planned to extinguish him. Why would you want him alive?"

Hiding emotions came easily, but she'd never

experienced positive ones so strongly before. "He's become a valued member of the crew."

"And? Even the most valued are sometimes not worth the trouble."

She leaned forward and cut the ropes keeping her brother secure in an effort to build trust. Still wielding the knife, she stepped back, edging her bottom onto the desktop. "Are you sure about that, brother? Solid crewmen are becoming increasingly difficult to find. Especially ones worth anything."

"Except, that one," Luther pointed behind her, "isn't worth much. I paid a small fortune to get him out of New Orleans, and for what? His ability to charm men into giving up a few secrets, and a collection of women's smiles after he's conned the panties off them."

The mercenary paused then, sitting forward in the chair and bracing his forearms on the arm pads. "Wait a minute. Is that what he's done to earn your endearment?" He turned in his chair, his scrunched eyes honing in on her lover. "Did you defile my sister?"

Lies required quick thinking and stealth, but she normally faced problems with a blade and threats. Fear gripped her like a tight corset, choking her breath and chest. Air wouldn't enter her lungs. Nothing worked right, and then everything went black.

She jumped up seconds later, wiping away the cold water thrown in her face. "What the hell?"

"Indeed, what a girl you turned out to be." Luther held out a hand, and she grabbed it, moving to a standing position near the desk. "You fainted."

"I've never done such a thing in my whole life, and I'm not a girl."

"First time for everything. Like when you screamed at a spider?" Of course, he'd say something ridiculous, bringing up memories that had no place here.

"Where's Ian?" Screw her brother. She wanted the man she loved.

"Right here," he replied, pushing between her and Luther and wrapping his arms around her. "Do you feel okay?"

"Fine, but he can't kill you. I love you." *Damn it.* She was trembling now. She'd never wish these emotions on her worst enemy. The highs and lows they'd brought her—awful. Even more unpleasant, Luther could use this against them. Regret swamped her like a stomach bug, tensing her gut and frame.

"I don't think love will stop him, Sorella." He pressed a kiss to her head. She wanted the real deal, not some poor attempt at propriety.

"Really kiss me."

Through clenched teeth, he replied, "Now is not the place or the time."

"Do you love me or not?"

He pulled back, "What the hell kind of question is that? Of course I do. I wouldn't lie for just anyone. I murdered someone for you, actually put a blade in a body. I went to the damn British Embassy, risked arrest in my own hometown, all for you."

She smiled a silly stupid grin at the thought. He'd done all those things for himself, too. Except for killing a man. He'd protected her when he abhorred killing and knocked out her sibling so she wouldn't have to. Looking back on those situations gave her a renewed love for the man before her. He was in a class of his own, and he had done all that insane stuff to get her to this moment.

She'd have to end her brother if he didn't give Ian a pardon.

"You two? Really?" Luther dragged a hand through his beard. "I can't believe this. Sorella, are you really saying you love this merchant?" The word came out as an insult; no surprise since she'd been raised to marry a president's son.

"Yes, I do."

Luther picked Ian up by his neck. "Now answer my question. Did you defile my sister?"

"I can't—breathe." Once his feet touched the floor, her lover coughed and then responded, "I don't believe I'll answer that, but I love her and if she'll have me—granting you spare my life—I'll provide for her the best I can until the end of my days."

"Sounds an awful lot like a marriage proposal." Her brother looked back at her. "Do you accept it?"

"Uh, yes?" *What the hell is happening?*

"Then by the powers that be, you're man and wife."

He was free of Luther's deadly fingers around his neck, and Sorella kissed him as if it was the last time they'd get the opportunity. She pried his lips open, battling with his tongue until her brother cleared his throat, and she stepped back. No doubt they'd be up to much worse once they were alone, but he still didn't understand everything.

"You're a gang of mercenaries. How can you

marry people?"

"Airship captain?" He waved his hands in the air as if conjuring the answer.

Ian shook his head. "Meaning?"

His captain elbowed him. "We have authority to marry people."

"Really? Interesting, but what about my life?"

"You're my sister's husband. That doesn't mean I won't kill you, but since she wants to keep you around, I'll consider her trade." Now brother focused on sister. She freed herself of his arm and stepped up, ready for the challenge. Ian would never tell anyone how much it turned him on. Her tough exterior and her bravery were something fierce.

"You agree to spare his life now, or I end yours." His captain struck with the opening bid.

"My life, the soldier's, and the German ship."

"The German ship is no one's. It needs to be burned." She pointed out the window. "We have no idea what havoc is still to come from that ship following us. Best to cut losses and get out of here. The guards will be released at Europe's border. They only work to feed their families. Your life for my husband's, and you let my crew burn down the kaiser's experimental vessel."

Luther stroked his cheeks, beard included. "Fine. It's a deal. Consider it a wedding present."

Ian nearly laughed out loud. Of course, these two would find such things to be run of the mill—dealing in lives, men, and enemy war ships like they were pottery and fine cloth. Chalk this up to the craziest day ever, another adventure. Yet things were right in the world, and he'd found a bit of happiness for one day. Sorella was his wife. No matter how things went now, at least they were in it together, pledged to each other for better or worse.

Luther eyed them. "That doesn't mean I'm done with you, and, technically, you owe me at least a favor for making my life so damn difficult."

He pulled his wife to his side, loving how her words were perfect, and she was perfect nestled against him. Then they both spoke at the same time. "Name it."

***

Sorella stared out her cabin's porthole at the setting sun. Bastille and the crew had returned, and the orange sky burned a little brighter as the German ship sank toward the ocean. Her first mate also reported that Luther's refugee camp did indeed exist with plentiful food and no mistreated members. Some of her crew were even reunited with loved ones and had chosen to stay behind for a night.

Then she and Ian had dined with her brother—a wedding dinner, he'd called it, to celebrate their rushed, but desired, nuptials. Luther had accused her and Ian of already being an old married couple as they debated everything and nothing over the table. She had enjoyed the volatile nature of their relationship, though, had enjoyed being challenged.

Now on her wedding night, she waited in her chamber for her husband to join her. He'd stayed behind on Luther's vessel for one more drink, and she'd warned him he'd be locked out for taking too long. An empty threat, of course.

"Sorella," Ian called out, the cabin door creaking as it opened.

"I'm here by the window."

"Thank goodness. I was worried you'd run away as soon as you came to your senses." He shut the door behind him, and she heard his boots strike the floor as he crossed the room.

"Who says I'm not planning on it?"

He wrapped his arms around her waist and pulled her against him. "You're a tease, wife."

"And you love it." She turned in his arms, running her fingers through his hair, gripping tight and pulling him in for a kiss.

When they finally broke for air, she asked, "What did my thieving brother want to talk to you about?"

"Nothing to do with a job. Some things he'd found out, things we may want to concern ourselves with." He started in on her clothes, unbuttoning and tugging.

"What things?" She bent her arms to accommodate his actions, and her shirt came off, baring her bosom to the night.

"Do you ever wear undergarments?"

"In battle,"

He smiled. "Really? Otherwise, you're naked as a newborn under one layer of clothing?"

She nodded.

His mouth and deft fingers continued their assault on her breasts, but she thought his fingers could be put to much better use pleasuring her lower half.

"Hurry. I need you," she pleaded.

"As my captain commands." He worked her pants open and set to his task. Only a few minutes with those magic fingers, and she cried out his name.

As he bent her over the bed, face flat to the mattress, and plowed into her from behind, it took even less time for a second orgasm to crest. Then he joined her in completion, at last allowing himself release in her body. She knew his seed was filling her, possibly allowing her to bear his child, and pride surged through her. In their profession, childbearing would be dangerous, but, still, the idea lit a spark of joy in her and provided a content feeling she'd not known before. She whispered, "I love you," as he collapsed beside her.

Sometime later, after a few more rounds of lovemaking, they held each other. Moonlight flowed through the porthole and cast a strange glow throughout the room.

"We were talking about my brother and things?"

Ian lifted his head from her stomach, "Yes, things. His spies say the kaiser has signed an agreement to build a tunnel from France to England, but it's a plot to lull the two countries into a sense of false security. Because France and England have trade agreements with Germany, they'll welcome the tunnel. Once it's built, the kaiser plans to attack."

"Makes sense. He already tried to take England by air and sea. Those options didn't work out well." Sorella pushed aside the ball of fear taking up residence in her chest. Pretty soon, war would erupt everywhere. "Anything else?"

"Another debutante-raised-assassin is being put in place to marry the president's son."

"What?" The very thing she'd attempted to prevent with her disappearance was moving forward anyway. "How?"

"I don't know all the particulars, but Luther found out the kaiser has beautiful girls from every European country, daughters of men in political power raised similarly to you and ready to be deployed into enemy territory, so the wedding proceeds in six months. The announcement is expected any day."

"*Dio*. We have to do something."

Ian moved up beside her and pulled her into an embrace. She went willingly.

"That's not our assignment, sweet Sorella."

"Will it be someone's?" She hoped so. Hell, she'd talk to Luther about it tomorrow.

"I don't know. For now, I'm going to grab some happiness and worry about the problem later. It's our wedding night, not the end of the world."

Sorella pressed a soft kiss to his lips. "For the moment, you're right…. This time."